Fae Pursuit

Tangled Fae: Book Four
Sarah K. L. Wilson

Published by Sarah K. L. Wilson, 2020.

FAE PURSUIT

First edition. April 17, 2020.

Written by Sarah K. L. Wilson.

For Cale, always.

Other Books by Sarah K. L. Wilson

Creeping Darkness
Golem Siege
Memory of Mountains
Color of Victory
Dragon Tide Series
Dragonlet
Dragon Staff
Desperate Flight
Bubbles of Hope
Waves of Destiny
Tides of Change
Keys of Power
Rock Eaters
Underworld
Chosen One
The Unweaving Chronicles Series
Teeth of the Gods
Lightning Strikes Twice
Thunder Rattles High
Bridge of Legends Series
Summernight
Dawnspell
Autumngale
Winterfast
Springhatch
Tangled Fae Series
Fae Hunter
Fae Captive
Fae Nightmare

BOOK ONE

Tha-thrum, Tha-thrum, their feet the drum,
They leap, they chase, they flee, they run.
Down where the dozy daisies drift,
Up over rocky heights and cliffs,
Leap from the cliff to heed the call,
Dance from snapping slathering jaws,
Dart from tear of teeth and claws,
Hope for daybreak, distant long,
Alike they fall, both weak and strong,
Laugh, dead creatures, laugh and play,
Dance and wheel until the day.
Songs of the Faewald

Chapter One

DUSK SETTLED AROUND us as I stepped from the human world to the Faewald. Will-o-the-wisps danced erratically through the descending charcoal of near-night. I clung to the sword with one hand and Scouvrel with the other.

"I'm already in your power, Nightmare," he said dryly. "You need hardly clutch me to you like a trinket you fear will be stolen."

Behind us, the tear in the air closed and I let out a sigh I'd been holding in.

"I killed him," I said tightly.

"Yes, Nightmare," Scouvrel said, bending to peer down into my cage before looking back up at me. "You delivered the Great Insult to The Balance. The last reminder that even we – who are nearly immortal – are not fully immortal. Neither pestilence nor starvation may lay us waste, and yet a broken arrow in the hands of the furious Hunter will sever us just as fully. And yet, it is an insult which has left you in a precarious situation."

"I hardly think so," I said confidently. "I've stolen you back, and my sister, too."

From within the cage, I heard a hiss.

"Am I your loot, then, Pirate? Your stolen treasure?" Scouvrel asked, amused.

"You are many things," I said, scowling. "Friend, ally, husband, betrayer, and captor but hardly something so passive as a treasure."

"You're beginning to sound like him," my sister said from the cage. "That's not a good sign. I was shocked when I heard you married the Knave. How utterly unlike you."

I ignored her. I would deal with her later.

"Where are we, Knave?" I asked Scouvrel – or perhaps I should think of him as Finmark since that was his true name. It seemed prudent to keep that to myself. The only other person who'd heard me say it out loud was The Balance and he was dead now.

"These are the Hummingdales," he said, looking around us. We were on the top of a round hill, the earth falling away from us in every direction. Tufts of long grass blew in the balmy winds – too hot for me in my winter clothing – and vines as thick as my arms crept along the ground and around the hill, bearing blooms so large that Scouvrel and I could slip into one together with no one the wiser. Now, why had I thought of that?

The heady fragrance of the blossoms filled the air, and large hummingbirds – as large as I was – fluttered from one to the next, darting in to drink their nectar.

"I wonder how long it has been since I was here last," I mused.

"It's a single day since I was last here," Hulanna said from the cage. "The Blood Moon is still rising. See the delicate rim of red along the bottom of it? Blood will slowly fill the moon through this whole moon cycle. And now that we have established our location and date, I would like to negotiate my release."

I lifted the cage to look at my sister and she flung out her hand dramatically at me as if she was throwing something at my eye. Nothing happened. I lifted an eyebrow.

"Trying to practice magic on me, sister?" I asked, holding her cage out far enough that she couldn't endanger me. "Don't think for a moment that I trust you. I watched you slay your husband with my own eyes. I watched you march an army of Fae to our village – to our home! I watched you torture my father. My trust is very thin."

She hissed, slipping from the back of her frantic stag. He attacked the bars of the cage again, hitting them with bone-shattering blows. It was never peace and harmony in there, was it? All my "guests" except for the children seemed to want nothing more than to murder every living thing.

"Enough," I said between clenched teeth. I couldn't leave my sister anywhere or I'd risk losing her, but I needed to talk to Scouvrel and I wanted privacy. I set the cage down on the ground and pulled off my quiver and then my coat so I could cover the cage with it.

Scouvrel's eyebrows were raised by the time I looked up again.

"We need to talk, and I don't want her commenting," I explained.

Scouvrel looked up at the slowly rising moon. "If you wish to converse, you should speak quickly."

"You said we were enemies now," I said tightly. He couldn't tell I was nervous, could he?

He nodded. "You are now the Leveler. Righter of wrongs. Destroyer of worlds."

"What does that mean?" I insisted.

He leaned in very close and I leaned in, too. Perhaps he planned to tell me something too secret to share with Hulanna. Perhaps ...

He kissed me so suddenly, so desperately, so violently, that I gasped. I could taste blood on my lip from where his teeth had grazed the delicate flesh. When he pulled away, his expression was agonized, his eyes too bright.

"Dearest Nightmare, you will shatter me. You will destroy me. You will break every shard of me and crush it to powder."

What was he talking about?

"That other Balance didn't do those things," I protested.

"We are two sides of the coin – my role is to sow chaos and yours to bring order, just as the Sooth's job is to bring enlightenment and insight and the Kinslayer to bring confusion and entanglement."

"I already told you," I said firmly – firmly because now he was scaring me. "I don't take any role that I don't choose. I haven't chosen to be the Balance. I don't have one white wing and one dark wing or one dark half of my hair and one light half. I'm not bound and determined to do evil, or to make things balanced, or to enslave you, or to trick anyone!"

"You cannot resist, horrible Nightmare," he whispered, laying a light kiss on my hair as his fingers squeezed my arms far too tightly. "You cannot play any other role now. We are separated forever like the sun and the moon, the day and the night, the fish and the bird. From afar I may admire and honor you, but never again can we be one."

"We weren't one to begin with," I grumbled.

He only stared at me with eyes as deep as a fresh-dug well.

"You took my hand. You gave me the frog. Are you saying that you will not offer me your blood next?"

Was that the next part of the agreement that confirmed our marriage? I shivered. It was always blood for the Fae. Couldn't they think of anything else? Couldn't I bake him bread or make him a set of fine arrows? No, it had to be blood.

I'd fulfilled those two signs without meaning to. I'd agreed to our marriage without meaning to. I shouldn't be agreeing at all.

It wasn't right to marry a Fae. It was a sign of accepting their world, of allowing them in, or somehow tacitly approving of their horrors. And I couldn't do any of those things. I should tell him now that I was done with him. That I did not care to finish the ceremonial actions or to confirm anything, that I was his betrayer as much as he was mine.

I felt my expression hardening. I felt the words forming on my tongue. I needed to be bold. I needed to do what I must. There should be no misunderstandings.

Something flickered in his eyes – something vulnerable and raw. I shut my jaw with a snap.

"Just because the Faewald says I am a thing," I said, crossing my arms over my chest, "doesn't mean that's true. I choose what roles I fill. And I am *not* the Balance."

A flicker of a sardonic smile fluttered around the edge of his lips. "Then why, dearest Nightmare, is one of your eyes suddenly green and the other brown?"

I gasped. What was he talking about? I fumbled for my mirror but it was back with my bag. Had my eyes really changed color?

"As much as your discomfiture brings me great delight," Scouvrel said, standing up on his toes, his wings of charcoal smoke springing out from his shoulders. "You must retrieve your things – and quickly. I can feel another of us close by and that can only mean one thing."

"What does it mean?" I asked, snatching my jacket from Hulanna's cage and pulling it back on.

"The sound of horns, the chase of heels, the pounding of the heart, and the end of dreams most precious," he whispered, snatching my hand from the air and kissing the tips of my fingers with aching eyes.

But I knew better than to be charmed by that. I knew better than to trust him again. He might claim friendship and shared goals. But in the end, he was as bound to cruelty as any Fae. If I was going to best him and them, then I must begin to think like them and make my heart as hard as ice.

Chapter Two

I BARELY HAD MY QUIVER over my shoulder and the cage tied to my belt when a horn pierced the air. It sounded like a wolf howl mixed with the tumbling longing of a pipe.

"I thought there was no music in the Faewald," I gasped.

My sister snickered in a way that made me want to stab my knife through the bars of the cage. I ignored her.

"That's no music, haunting Nightmare," Scouvrel said, eyes sharp as he scanned the horizon. His sewing needle was back in his hand. "They ride."

"Why do you keep that needle?" I asked. "Surely there must be better swords in the Faewald."

"Even I am allowed a moment of sentiment once in a millennium, wouldn't you say, Nightmare? Or do you wish to rob me of this singular joy?"

"I have never stolen anything from you but your freedom – and I gave that back."

"Lies fall from your lips like fragrant oil, you horrible Nightmare. You have stolen things you don't realize you took." I couldn't tell if that was affection or derision in his tone. "But now we must run or forfeit our lives."

"Run from what?" I asked. "Are you afraid that the Fae will chase me here because I am the Balance now?"

"They will not just chase you here, Nightmare. They will chase you *everywhere* until you have killed so many of them that the blood flows in rivers across the Faewald. But it is not that from which we run now. As long as the Blood Moon marks the sky, the Wild Hunt is called. That sound you heard announced its arrival. The dead chase us now and those we have killed are hot on our heels, seeking to drag us back with them to the world behind the Dread Doors. Which means we must flee until dawn or until we can find an earth-marked door to shelter us."

That didn't sound good.

"Bargain with me, Nightmare – one last time."

Why did the word "last" feel so painful?

"What do you want to bargain for?" I asked.

"Let me fly you to safety tonight," he said with a heart-melting look in his eyes. "In exchange for my name."

But I didn't want to give him his name back. Not when it was the only power I had. I didn't understand him at all – not the beatings he'd taken to keep me safe nor why he'd married me, nor even why he'd betrayed me. Because no matter what he said about being forced into it, he'd still *done* it. And I would never do such a thing to someone I cared about. I'd find another way.

Worse than that. I didn't like the way my heart seemed to beat too quickly around him – as if he was giving me a fever, or how I couldn't seem to be cured of him – as if he was a disease unto death.

There had to be a way to fight how that made me feel, and his name was the only weapon I had.

"I don't think so," I said, sprinting down the hill toward the Blood Moon, my feet flying down unfamiliar landscape.

Don't trip, Allie. Don't trip. You'll really look like a fool if you do!

The cage rattled in my hand. My sister must be hitting the bars with every stride.

"You're running the wrong way!" Scouvrel said with a scowl as he caught up to me. He still hadn't buttoned his shirt and as the breeze caught it, exposing his torso, I saw the wounds and thorn tattoos – wounds from where he bore pain for me and thorns from when he married me against my will – just like the feathers I bore now on my arms – marks of him that intermingled with my own. Could it be possible to become tangled up with another person so that you could no longer tell what was hurting them and what was hurting you? To the point where their interests became your interests and their future your future?

"Then show me the right way," I said, pushing all my strength into every stride. It felt good to channel my frustration into running. Pumping each desperate thought into my pace as I went. "Show me where to go and what to do. Be my ally again. Don't tell me this is the last time. Don't tell me we are enemies and opponents and fated to destroy each other. Don't – "

My feet swept out from under me and my heart leapt into my throat. I gasped, searching for the threat, but we were in the air, borne up by Scouvrel's wings. He clutched me to his chest, his face inches from mine, his expression furious as he leaned in and pressed his forehead to mine.

"Stop asking for the impossible, Nightmare. Haunt me all you want. Haunt me until food becomes tasteless and wine less heady than water, but do not torture me with hope."

Out there somewhere, were my parents and hundreds of children who needed me. Out there somewhere, was a war between Fae and mortals that needed to be stopped. And my only ally was pretending that fate had severed us. There *was* one thing I wanted enough to give up my power over him. Though I was a fool to want it.

"Promise me it doesn't matter – that roles or not, you will fight with me, you will champion me," I said, letting my fingers drift to his wounds. He flinched as I ran a finger along an open gash in his shoulder. "You bore this for me. Don't tell me it was for nothing. Pledge yourself to me and I will return to you your name."

He shook his head, pained at my offer.

"Don't be a fool, Allie," Hulanna hissed. "If you have his name and you truly are the Balance, then you have everything. Together, we can rule the Faewald and the Mortal world combined. Don't give it up for a pretty pair of eyes. Don't make the mistake I made."

"I can't make a promise I can't keep," Scouvrel hissed, as if he were in pain.

"I can't be married to a man who won't make that promise."

The horns behind us sounded again and then Scouvrel plunged toward the ground.

"Are you hurt?" I gasped.

"He can only fly for a little while during the hunt," Hulanna said condescendingly. "You expect to conquer us and yet you don't even know the basic rules of the Faewald. You're such a small-town mortal, Allie. It's pathetic. If you knew anything at all, you'd know that the Wild Hunt sucks the magic out of the Faewald, rendering us weakened as we run. Your fool of a husband shouldn't have wasted what he had to impress you."

"I think your tongue is too sharp, Lady of Cups," Scouvrel cooed as we landed, smacking a huge white blossom as we struck the ground. My bones felt jarred by our sudden landing, but Scouvrel didn't even stop talking. "Perhaps if I fed you one of your own ears it would take the edge off."

"I doubt you can, Knave," Hulanna shot back. "My resemblance to my sister is still there despite my advanced beauty and immortality. Could you bear to listen to me scream with her same voice? Could you stand the torment of watching my pain show in her same eyes?"

He snickered, but his laugh had an edge that made me nervous.

The horn sounded again – closer.

"What happens if we don't run?" I asked, my voice more tremulous than I liked.

"We turn to stone," Hulanna said. "'*Rooted to the earth you'll be as your cowardice rooted your feet from flight.*' That's one of the rules. So, run my frail mortal sister. Run until your feet bleed."

She didn't need to tell me twice.

Earlier in the Faewald...

HE'D BEEN WAITING FOR her to come. When she finally walked through the doors to where he was hanging in a silk bag, he could feel her there – waiting, choosing her words carefully.

"I've always thought that the Knave had the best role," she said smoothly.

A knife pierced the red silk, just inches from his nose. He drew back, dodging the knife as it slid down through the silk bag and spilled him on the floor.

He leapt to his feet, gasping, gratefully, at the cold air, his muscles and joints feeling as if they might give out at any moment. How long had he been contained within it? It had felt like years.

Dank sweat dried on him as the air around them swirled.

"Well?" she asked, lifting a perfect brow.

"As you say, Lady," he croaked. He could feel his power swelling up just beyond the stone circle he stood within.

"I could let you out of that circle," she said, toying with the gown she wore – a gown made entirely of white glass beads. The beads were tied at the neckline over a shoulder and again across the hips. The stretching and hanging of the beads made them rattle and shiver when she moved.

He tried not to betray his excitement, but he couldn't stop himself from licking his lips.

"Bargain with me," she cooed. "Bargain with me for your life."

He swallowed.

"What is your offer, Lady of Cups?"

She ran her fingers through her soft red hair as if she was only now considering this bargain – as if she hadn't been thinking it up for days while he stewed in his own sweat and agony.

"Hunt my sister. Find her and bring her to the Faewald," she cooed.

"And?" he asked.

"Merely that."

"And what will I receive?"

"I will release you from your burden – from the debt you owe, and the tie placed on you. You will be free and clear."

"Agreed," he said through a hoarse throat. "I agree to your bargain."

She'd already made her first mistake. She hadn't specified what he would do once he had her sister. And he already had a plan for that.

Chapter Three

WE SPRINTED DOWN THE hill, darting around curling green vines and soft fluttering petals, ducking and weaving around the buzz of panicked hummingbirds, darting lightning-fast past us. Will-o-the-wisps, glowing magenta or soft teal or bright yellow, fluttered in the air, gathering into ever larger and larger swarms as if there was safety in numbers for them, just like for us.

There were statues scattered across the open ground – like an artist had run wild, erecting sculptures with no regard to who might view them. They were Fae – of course – exactly life-sized and depicted with looks of terror on their faces. He clearly had a favorite expression.

One nearby looked almost identical to the woman I'd seen at the Court of Wings' party – the one with the owl sewn to the shoulder of her dress. Her eyes were wide in the depiction, her lips parted in horror.

My feet pounded over the mossy turf, my heart galloping in my chest and my lungs straining to breathe fast enough as my legs screamed at me to slow down. I dare not stop. Scouvrel kept his pace to mine as we crested the next rise and I stole a look behind my back.

When he'd claimed the dead were chasing us, I hadn't believed him, but the ghastly army of shades proved me wrong. They rode on flickering mounts – foxes and stags, unicorns and phoenixes, hounds and lynx, running birds I had no name for

– and even a snake with a body thicker than our goat shed. On each back rode one or two or even five of the dead. They were nearly transparent, but outlined in chalky hues and even from far away, I saw their hands were bristling with weaponry.

I gasped at the sight of one of them. His wings were far too familiar – one a dark batwing and one a bright white-feathered wing of a bird. The old Balance. Scouvrel had been telling the truth – our dead were hunting us.

At their forefront, ran a pack of pale blue specters of dogs. Each one was larger than the cottage I was raised in. Their chests were broad and muscles rippling. Moonlight glinted off the fangs of the nearest one. They ran, spirit drool flying from their slathering mouths.

Mounted on one of the dogs was a massive figure, horned like a ram and shirtless. His body bore rows of thorns like a rose bush, which started small at the neck and grew as large as claws as they reached his knuckles and the waistband of his pants. A long tail with a hook on the end trailed behind him, slashing through the air as if something was agitating him. His skin was blue as skimmed milk, but his eyes glowed an unearthly orange. Blue tattoos swirled in loops around his thorny skin and his head was shaved up to a swath that ran down the center of his head, plaited into a long sleek braid that split when it reached his shoulder into four equal plaits like the end of a whip. His long, pointed Fae ears bore a dozen ivory rings.

I could have sworn his eyes met mine across the distance.

I shuddered at the sight.

"Wait," I gasped. "We can go between worlds. Let me draw my sword."

"Not during the Wild Hunt," Scouvrel gasped. He didn't look taxed, and yet his breath came quickly. "No magic will work during the Hunt unless you've stored it."

"I have to try!" I drew the sword and slashed the air. Again. Again.

Nothing.

Cursing, I jammed the sword back into my belt just in time for Scouvrel to grab my hand and drag me after him.

"Run little cockroach," my sister called to me. "Run, run, run!"

"Be quiet," I snarled at her. "You're in no position to gloat."

"Aren't I? You captured me and yet you did not win. The prophecy is not fulfilled. My armies still roam the mortal world. What can you possibly do now?"

I ignored her, though a stab of fear shot through me. I couldn't dwell on how accurate her words were – not right now.

The horns sounded again sending fresh chills down the backs of my legs.

"This way," Scouvrel panted.

"Can we ride something, too?" I gasped.

"If we can find something. Everything will be running. Fae and beast. They'll destroy any they can catch, turning us to stone or dragging us to the Dread Door."

Those statues ... the ones with terror in their eyes ... had they been the ones that were turned to stone?

"What's the Dread Door?"

My sister began to laugh – a spooky, maddening laugh. "Tell her, Knave. Tell her about the Dread Door. Tell her about what will happen if the Wild Hunt gets her."

Scouvrel's expression was hard as stone as he tugged me through the satin blossoms. Eerie shadows danced across his face as the petals danced and rippled in the breeze.

"Ignore the Lady of Cups, Nightmare. I know a place not far from here. We must be fleet of foot and strong of heart, but we'll be fast enough if we put these delays to an end. Or would you rather ride in the Hunt the next time the horn sounds and chase me as the former Balance now chases you?"

"You noticed that?" I asked, frustrated when my voice came out as a squeak.

"He hunts me, too," Scouvrel growled. "All my dead do. And there are so very many of them. I am no shining knight, little Hunter. I am death and terror. I am what makes the shadows jump and hide."

"No," I said firmly. "That's what I am. That's what Hunters are."

"Oh please, save your bragging for when we're safe from the Hunt," Hulanna said.

I shook her cage roughly, smiling at her hiss of pain. And then I froze.

"Nightmare?" Scouvrel asked. "Are you injured?"

I shook my head, running on, but I was horrified by that impulse inside myself – that sweet joy that filled me when I tasted revenge. Was that new? Had that come with my new 'role'?

I'd always believed we were the sum of our choices. And I'd been choosing right – or at least trying to – until now. That had to count for something, didn't it? *Didn't it?*

We tumbled down a hill, skidding and slipping over loose earth and to a small creek flowing between night-blooming lilies, their white petals stained red by the rising Blood Moon. In front of us, surprised into stillness, a pair of ghastly foxes as big as horses stood, their backs choked with seven of the dead.

Scouvrel's fingers dug into my hand and then we were running down the creek, the water splashing around us in angry spurts, soaking my breeches, spraying up to coat face and hands. I spared a look at my feet and had to look back up again. Ghastly hands rose from the water, blue and flickering as if they weren't quite real. They snatched at our feet with every step.

Hulanna screamed from the cage. She'd have to endure with the rest of us.

My breath came in ragged gasps and I tasted blood in the back of my mouth. I couldn't run any faster.

The breath of something huge sounded like it was right against my neck. It had to be those giant dogs. I could almost feel specks of their hot slather spattering against me.

Every sense of mine was flooded with so much sensation that I couldn't separate one from another. Terror tried to choke me, seizing my screaming muscles, throttling my pounding heart, choking out the breath I gasped for. With a mental surge, I forced it away.

Fuel, Allie. This is your fuel!

My feet ran faster. My mind focused as sharp as an arrow hurtling to the target. I was fast. I was lightning. I was the rays of the sun. I was ...

Something scraped across my back, searing me with pain. A scream tore from my lips, unbidden. I tumbled toward the ground, but something seized me before I hit it.

Chapter Four

DARKNESS FILLED MY vision. But I was conscious. We'd stepped into a shadow. Something creaked as a door was flung open – a door with a dark streak of mud across it. The door smacked the wall with a crash. And then everything felt cool, as if we were under the earth. Another crash and the door was shut behind us. Something banged. Was Scouvrel barring the door?

I blinked back savage pain. Too much pain. Too much.

Scouvrel was cursing.

And then light filled the room.

He held up a lantern full of will-o-wisps. They fought and hooted at one another, growing brighter the more they fought. The room wavered in their shifting light.

Scouvrel stood over me with one hand extended, his face focused, concentrating. He bit his lip.

"Nightmare," he said cautiously. "How are you ... feeling?"

"Like something swiped claws across my back," I growled. "What hit me? Was it the fox?"

He didn't answer. He simply took the cage from my hand, untangling it from my belt and setting it on a low table. My sister was on the edge of the cage peering through the bars with bright, hungry eyes. She looked excited – too excited. I flinched from the sight.

Scouvrel swallowed, carefully removing my bow and quiver.

"Can you trust me tonight, Nightmare? Trust me with your life for just a few hours?"

Could I? The last time I trusted him, he hit me from behind and put me in that very cage.

He reached down and carefully removed my sword, speaking to me calmly, like you might to an injured child.

"We're safe here in this cairn. The long earth is marked with the clay of the mortal world. It's a safe place on a Blood Moon night. We can harbor here until daylight."

I tried to speak, but my mind was foggy, my words slipping between my fingers.

"My back hurts," I managed, fighting through the pain.

"And now we come to the first fork in the river, Nightmare," Scouvrel said, his lip curling suggestively. "On the one hand, a steep drop over a waterfall. On the other hand, a dark cavern with no end in sight, and which will you choose, I wonder? How much of your humanity will you gamble for power?"

"All of it," Hulanna opined from her cage. "She's my twin. She'll make my choice."

Scouvrel's eyebrow rose and a secretive smile stole over his face. "Care to place a bet, Lady of Cups?"

"Certified by the Balance?" she quipped, standing a little straighter so that her figure was enhanced by her posture. Was she flirting with my husband? Really?

"If it pleases you," Scouvrel said. "The loss, I admit, will not be mine."

She laughed, a silky, cunning laugh and I felt a growl building in my throat. That was *my* Scouvrel she was laughing with in that seductive, syrupy fashion.

"I'll wager you my best set of emerald earrings that she'll take the power," Hulanna offered.

"Now, now, Lady." Scouvrel's smile deepened. "You can do better than that."

Hulanna's laugh tinkled as she sat down on the white stag who filled the bottom of the cage, sleeping.

"Fine. I will wager the Smoke Falls to your Eye of the Knave," she said. "Worth playing for?"

"Yes," he said, almost hissing with delight. He turned his bright eyes to me. "Choose now, Nightmare, where you will roam. In the next hour, the choice will be made and there's no going back."

"What am I choosing?" I asked thickly. The pain was unbearable.

His eyes danced with clever wariness mixed with delight. It was easy to forget that despite his sweet words, he gained energy from my emotion – any emotion, even terror and pain.

"The agony in your back was not from the attack of the Wild Hunt, though they nearly snatched you from me. It's the beginning of the manifestation of your new role. Your skin has rent along your shoulder blades. If you do nothing, wings will grow there overnight – wings that match those of the former Balance, if I'm not mistaken. His predecessor had similar wings before he took the role from her and grew his own."

I shivered, imagining a batwing and angel wing on my back. Imagining being a creature of the Faewald instead of my mortal home.

Imagining, too, flying all on my own from place to place. I liked flying with Scouvrel. I'd like it even more if I could do it independently. I clenched my jaw as the temptation took hold, mixing with a primal horror that wrenched my guts and tugged.

"But you don't have to make that choice," Scouvrel said silkily. "I have thread and a needle in a little purse in my pocket. I can stitch up your skin. And if I do that, there will be no wings. And your skin will heal once again."

"How do you know?" I gasped.

His nose nearly brushed mine he was so close now, his eyes glittering with suppressed emotion. "Because I made this very choice myself."

I swallowed down a lump in my throat. And it had cost him, hadn't it? That's what their bet was about. It had cost him his humanity in some small way to gain the power of flight. Had it been worth it?

He licked his lips nervously.

It didn't matter whether it had been worth it to him or not. It only mattered what it would mean to me. It would mean accepting this role. Choosing to let the fates of the Fae determine my future. Or, it would mean remaining fully human, remaining fully the Hunter, remaining one of my people.

It was an easy choice.

"Stitch me up," I said hoarsely.

My sister hissed in her cage, but Scouvrel's delighted laugh gave me a warm feeling in my belly. He winked at me.

"You've just won me a delightful prize, Nightmare. I should put all my wagers on you in the future."

"Haven't you already?" Hulanna asked.

Scouvrel scoffed, but I couldn't see his face as he reached for his pocket. I let my eyes close against the pain. It wasn't losing something to give up what you'd never had to begin with. It really wasn't.

"And now that is settled," my sister said from her cage, "I would like to strike a bargain with my twin sister."

Earlier in the Faewald ...

"BARGAIN WITH ME, SCOUVREL of the Court of Wings," the Knave said, training his crossbow on Scouvrel. The dart flashed in the light of the will-o-wisps dancing around the pond in the velvety darkness. "Why die without at least trying to bargain?"

"A bargain with you is a death sentence all its own," Scouvrel said coolly as he snatched a fish from the stream, lifted it up and bit its neck. He devoured it, fresh, with all the look of enjoying the disgusting meal. "Why bargain without at least the threat of death?"

"Life is a bargain," the Knave said, as he leaned over the edge of the pool. "The only question is what terms the bargain will have. I was summoned here to collect the head tax from you."

Scouvrel froze.

"Yes. Maverick of the Court of Silk knows what you did. He knows you freed his plaything. The one with the curling auburn hair. Now, why would you do such a thing?"

"Why would you care? You aren't the Kinslayer."

The Knave shrugged. "I don't care. And it's not my job to go around collecting head taxes for stolen mortals. But when Maverick was foolish enough to summon me and request this, I saw an opportunity."

"Of course you did."

The look in Scouvrel's eye was bored, but there was just a hint of too much curiosity behind the boredom.

The Knave smiled wickedly. "Your brother keeps a tight Court. I mean to change that. Bring him to me instead, and I'll handle your debt to the Court of Silk."

"If I slaughter my brother everyone will suspect me. After all, I'm next in line as Lord of Wings," Scouvrel said, throwing what was left of the fish on shore and wading up onto the bank.

The hands of the dead clawed at his feet as he walked, but he ignored them stoically, pulling his clothing from where they hung on a lovely white marble statue of a fae with deer antlers crowning her head. He began to dress.

"That's of no concern to me," the Knave said. "Or rather, it's exactly what I'm hoping for. In fact, I have a rare poison I'd like you to use. Felicitous Root."

He held up a small pink vial.

"Why that – specifically?" Scouvrel asked, donning his breeches and boots.

"You know how it kills – with so much pleasure you drown in it. And it's how he killed Lady Jerica."

Scouvrel's face was hard as a stone.

"When he senses he is dying by the same poison," the Knave said, dropping the tip of the crossbow to hold out the vial. "He'll know he died by my hand. Revenge, my dear Scouvrel, is sweeter than honey and the blood of mortals."

His eyes glittered and his crossbow fell further to point at the ground.

Scouvrel moved like an uncoiling snake, striking fast and hard. He grabbed the crossbow with one hand and the vial with the other, wrenching the crossbow away and flinging it into the pond even as he snatched the vial with the other hand.

The Knave's mouth opened in shock and Scouvrel smashed the vial against his teeth. Pink brighter than fuchsia flowers dripped from the Knave's teeth into his mouth.

He gasped, and then giggled.

Scouvrel's bitter sneer never changed. He grabbed the other fae's wrists holding him in place.

"Why would you do that?" the Knave said between laughter. His breath was coming too fast, his pupils completely dilated so his eyes looked black. "No one wants this role."

"It was better than the alternative," Scouvrel said quietly as the Knave's laughter rang out in ripples again and again.

"It's not," he said, gasping. "It's worse than anything."

He began to shake, his face a vision of rapture. His eyes rolled back into his head and he collapsed, spasmed, and went still.

Scouvrel's shoulders slumped.

He looked in one direction and then the other and then took the body and threw it in the pond.

Chapter Five

"GOOD," I SAID THROUGH heavy curtains of pain. "We should bargain, you and I, sister. You should have offered me a bargain before all this began – before you dragged me into this horrible world you were so bound and determined to embrace. What made you dance around those stones? What inspired you to drag me along with you?"

My words cut off with a groan as Scouvrel ripped my coat and shirt right down the back. The sound of tearing fabric left me shivering.

"Easy on the clothing, Knave," I said between gritted teeth. "Or you'll have to stitch that, too."

"I had no idea you had so many freckles, you ghastly thing," he said, ignoring me. "You're as speckled as an egg."

"Truth or lie?" I answered, biting my lip as his needle dug in again. "You're only commenting on my freckles because you're terrible at stitching."

"We're still playing that game? How delightful." His chuckle bubbled out in genuine delight. "Truth. Your back will be pinched and seamed like a poorly darned sock."

Well, that was a great visual.

"Well, Hulanna?" I asked, turning my attention back to my sister and flinching as Scouvrel's needle pulled at my flesh. "What made you do it?"

"What made me seek immortality?" she asked, rolling her beautiful eyes and running her fingers through her springy curls as if to mock me with their perfection. "What fool wouldn't seek it? I found a book that I wasn't supposed to find. They hid it down the well, those old fool women. Did you know, Allie, that mother and all the old Goodies of Skundton are like a secret society? Just the women. They don't tell the men." She laughed nastily. "And what they're protecting is the secret – the secret of the Faewald – they all know it. They pretend that they don't but they do. They could all be Fae. They could all be glorious. But, of course, they're too small-minded for that. They're intent on protectionism instead, on walls and rules and lies. Fools! I crept out at night, and while mother and father were terrified that I was trysting with village boys, I was actually reading that little book. I put it back when I was done – you could go find it yourself if you wanted to – and that was when I made up my mind to come to the Faewald and to bring you with me."

"So, all that doe-eyed enchantment you pretended to feel when Lord Cavariel arrived was just an act?" I asked. But it couldn't have been an act. Even I had been attracted to him.

"Not entirely," Hulanna said, her perfect Fae face coloring slightly as she broke eye contact with me. "Glamor works so well on mortals. And I was still mortal then."

"And did you agree to become Fae?" I asked quietly as Scouvrel tugged roughly against the thread on my back. When this was done, I would pay a village girl to teach him to sew. A child of eight would do better.

A haunted terror passed over her face before she spoke. She couldn't lie now. She seemed to be struggling to find the right words.

"I dreamed of becoming Fae from the moment I read of their power in that little book."

"That doesn't mean that you let them perform The Glory on you willingly. All it means is that you were a fool."

She sneered at me. "I've given you all the answers you need. I've told you that I was no poor victim – that I chose this life. I created this power for myself. I am Lady of Cups with no irritating Lord to hold me back. And I will rule as High Queen of all the Faewald. You could have reigned with me if you hadn't been so small-minded. If you'd come with me rather than running away and hitting your head on a rock."

I swallowed. She said it because it was true in her mind. But that didn't make it entirely true, did it? Maybe she had chosen that life. But she'd also been too foolish to know what she was choosing before it was chosen. She'd been both victim and perpetrator, both trapped and the trapper. And even now, I could sense she was setting a noose for me. If only I could understand what the trap would be.

She should be begging me for her freedom. She was the one in the cage. So why did I feel like she was still controlling things even from inside that cage?

Scouvrel moved to the other side of my back – just over my shoulder blade, his touch oddly gentle though his needlework still pulled and pinched.

"I think you've mistaken me for someone who doesn't have you trapped in a cage, sister," I said as the stag lying under her yawned, shaking his antlers and making Hulanna frown as she dodged them. "You aren't actually immortal just because you are Fae. If I am so inclined, I can throw your cage in a pool of water until you drown, or set it in a fire and let you burn."

Scouvrel's hands froze mid-stitch. Had I surprised him?

"You won't," Hulanna said with a smirk. "Not good-girl Al-lie. Not our father's favorite. You wouldn't dare disappoint him or that stupid stinking town. I've had years to think about this, Allie. Years to plan this. Do you really think I didn't spend that time thinking about you, too? I have a plan for you."

"I know all about your plan," I said through gritted teeth. "You need to 'win' me to secure your victory over the mortal world."

She hesitated, doubt clouding her eyes for a single heart-beat before her expression smoothed over. "Not to conquer the mortal world, Allie. I can do that on my own. In fact, my armies are doing that as we waste time here stitching your back. No, I need to win you to make the mortal world part of the Faewald. Then we will no longer be limited by stone circles or blood moons or iron. Then all the world will be the Faewald."

I shivered.

"You want to drag us all to hell?" I asked. Fury made my voice huskier than I'd prefer.

"I want to offer you heaven," she said with a serene smile. "The heaven of no more toil, no more ugliness, just glamor and magic and golem servants. No more squalling babies or need-less toil. No more goats to herd or animals to hunt – at least not unless you want to hunt and then you can hunt whatever you like however you like – even the Knave there. That might be fun."

She winked.

"You know I'll never agree to that."

"And why not? When I can offer so much?"

I laughed, a nasty, cruel laugh I'd learned from them. "Because I read those prophecies, too. And now I have you in a cage. If 'win' meant 'capture' then the Faewald would already be conquered and you'd all be banished back to this place. But it hasn't meant that, has it? Which means that to 'win' me you'll have to do more than just capture me. You'll have to kill me."

Hulanna sucked in a wary breath, as if she hadn't expected me to figure that out. Oddly, so very oddly, Scouvrel was silent. He did not gasp or freeze – almost as if he'd always known this. He pulled at a stitch and I twitched in pain.

"And what did you expect?" I asked, putting a bite into my words. "Did you expect me to offer myself up as a goat for slaughter?"

Hulanna didn't wait a single beat.

"Yes," she said. "That's exactly what I expect. Because it's that or else watch us extinguish the life of every mortal. Everyone you know will die. Everyone you love, except me. Every child with big eyes and old woman with trembling hands. Will you really do that, Allie Hunter? Will you really be so selfish that you would save your own life at the cost of theirs?"

"They wouldn't be in danger if not for you!" I snarled.

"But they are," Hulanna said with a self-satisfied smile. "And it doesn't matter that you've put me in this cage. My plans are well-orchestrated. They can go on without me. I can just sit here on the back of this stag and wait. And eventually, you will come to me and beg me to come out of the cage and take your life." Her words turned slow and deliberate. "Because you are the Hunter. You always have been. Your role is to protect our village and you can't abandon that. You can't be faithless. Loyalty was bred into your bones and trained into your heart. Self-lessness was baked into your mind. I know you, Allie. I know you down to your marrow. You will do this. It's who you are. All I have to do is wait."

I sat up abruptly, realizing Scouvrel had finished stitching my back a few moments ago. I stumbled, the back of my shirt and coat still open and flapping in the breeze of my movement, toward an open door. I didn't care that it was dark. I needed to be away from her. I needed to be gone. Now.

Hulanna's laughter followed me.

"You know it's true, Allie. You are who you are."

I stumbled into the dark, musty room, my breath coming in sharp gasps.

It took a moment to get the waves of panic to stop, to calm my breath. To suck in great gasping gulps of the dank air. A low light filled the room as soft footsteps padded up from behind me. It was a bedroom with a lone bed and a large wardrobe and an empty fireplace. Thick brocade curtains covered a window, their mulberry shade stitched with depictions of smiling Fae ripping foxes in half. A large oval mirror was framed with a gilded edge of eyeless smiling faces.

Pain seared across my back, making me weep silently.

Behind me, Scouvrel whispered. "Possibility that she's right?"

"Five," I gasped.

I could feel his shudder in the air behind me.

"Didn't you realize that?" I asked. "Wasn't that why you were so quiet?"

"It does not suit my plans to see you die for the Mortal Court, Allie Hunter," he whispered ,and my real name sounded so strange on his lips that I turned to look at him. There wasn't a single sparkle of amusement in his grave eyes. And that alone made me taste acid on my tongue. I swallowed.

"Then who would you have me die for?" I asked sharply.

"The Fae, of course," he said. "But who would ever choose to die for us?"

Chapter Six

I RAIDED THE WARDROBE and found a close-fitting shirt with a ruffle of lace around the collar and a doublet jacket in a virulent purple with slashes of black down the breast. It closed with silver clasps shaped like bird skulls along one side of the doublet. The sleeves of the hip-length jacket had lizard skeletons entwined in silver stitching running up them, but the lizards appeared to be winged. Each one was biting the tail of the last. The Fae treated their clothing like everything else – they made them glamourous, gorgeous but always with a hint of violence underneath.

"Truth or lie," Scouvrel asked me from the doorway where his back was turned, so I could ease the shirt and jacket over the painful slashes he'd stitched for me. "You finally understand the depths of my depravity."

I let those words hang in the air. Did I know that? He could be even worse than I guessed.

I struggled with the doublet. I couldn't get my arms around without ripping the new stitches. They stung – but not as much as I expected.

He turned, suddenly. "Let me help you with that."

His hands were surprisingly light and graceful as he took the doublet from my hands and helped me ease it over my pained shoulders. His hooded eyes revealed nothing.

The arrow hadn't pierced his heart when I fired it at him. It had lodged in his arm. Every time I felt like I should accept how black-hearted he was, that thought bobbed up to the surface. What did the bow know that I did not?

I swallowed.

I needed to make a decision. I could choose to stop trusting him – and lose his company, his help, his wisdom.

Or choose to follow that arrow and trust him again. Even though he kept saying things about how he was going to kill me someday.

I took a deep breath. I'd just have to follow my gut.

"Lie," I said as I fastened the last bird skull fastener on the doublet. "The arrow did not kill you. And it pierces evil hearts."

I guess I'd chosen to trust him – with no bargain and no promise. The thought set my teeth on edge and my pulse racing. It was like jumping over a cliff and not knowing how far the drop was. It was like launching an arrow into a charging bear and watching as it kept on coming. It filled me with the excited terror of risk and chance.

"Does magic work inside the house during the Blood Moon?" I asked calmly.

Scouvrel nodded, his gaze darting away as if he was ashamed of something. "To some extent. I can't heal you tonight, if that's what you are hoping for. I used up too much trying to fly."

"Then I have some things to retrieve," I said.

I strode past him and back into the other room, collected my quiver, bow, and sword and drew the sword, snatching the cage with my sister up with one hand.

I paused.

"Whose house is this?" I asked Scouvrel.

"A minor Fae's," he said with a shrug. "Someone with terrible taste. There's not a book in the entire place."

I nodded, set my sword down for a moment, ignoring the pain in my back that brought tears to my eyes, and gingerly opened the cage door. Scouvrel gasped, but my hand shot into the cage and held my sister – struggling – in place as the other hand pulled the stag out. He was a liability.

I shut the cage door swiftly as the stag was instantly full-sized again. His breath puffing out in furious gusts and his hoof stomping the floor of the small house. The floorboards cracked.

He turned on us, his eyes blazing cherry red. Fast as I could, I grabbed the sword, slashed the air and leapt through, sword and all.

I landed on the turf of the Mortal World in the exact place I'd hoped, darting to the side to make room for Scouvrel to leap through the rip.

He sprinted through, his face tight with stress and then grabbed me, pulling me behind the rip in the air at the same moment that the stag leapt through, running full-speed through the forest of the mortal world and away from us. I gasped, pulling my blindfold up.

I hadn't expected the stag to follow. Maybe I should be less impulsive.

"Trying to get me killed?" Scouvrel said lightly.

"One," I said, my own breath shuddering. I'd expected him to take care of himself. He was clearly capable of doing that without my help.

I licked my lips nervously. It was day in the mortal world. And though this little nook in the forest was quiet, it was not far from Skundton where the Fae would be completing their conquest. I needed to be quick and silent. That stag might even make a good distraction.

"Follow me," I strode into the little cave I'd found during the Feast of Ravens, my hands searching in the dark for my pack. Please let it be here, please!

Relief flooded me as my free hand found the pack.

"You came all the way back for this?" my sister asked disgustedly. "I should just start screaming and see if anyone comes."

I slung the pack over my shoulders and tied the cage back to my belt. I already had the axe handle in my hand when distant cries began.

"Can anyone hear me? Anyone? Help!"

That voice! I knew that voice.

I was running before I realized it, dashing between trees and over rocks. Behind me, Scouvrel's curses could have turned the air blue.

The mortal world always looked strange to me after the Faewald, as if someone had painted it on canvas without much pigment to go around. Compared to the vibrant colors of the Faewald, it was drained of life.

Within minutes, I stumbled to a stop, my blindfold falling off one of my eyes, the other still covered. As always, it made me see almost double – half the real world and half the spirit world.

In the spirit world, a strange cage was suspended from a tree. The bars of the cage moved and shifted like living snakes. No – wait – they were snakes. Their hisses filled the air, sliding down my spine.

The eye that could see the real world couldn't see them at all. With that eye, all I could see was Olen, huddled in midair. He was battered and broken, one of his eyes swelled shut and his fancy tabard shredded and bloodstained. Dried blood crusted a wound in his scalp and his eyes were hollow.

"Allie!" he gasped and the flicker of hope in his eyes made my heart sink. If Olen was excited to see me, then things were truly bad here.

I swallowed, glancing around the glen for Fae. This seemed like a trap, with Olen as the bait.

"Nightmare," Scouvrel warned, his voice deep with extra meaning. "I warn you that if you interfere in this, you will be forced into something you will not like."

I shot him a venomous look. "Just because you don't like him doesn't mean he should be treated like this. No one should be treated like that."

He raised a single eyebrow. "Nevertheless."

That was all. No specifics. No pleading. Just a single word. I shook my head and reached into my bag for the golden key.

"I didn't think anyone was listening. I didn't think anyone would come," Olen said. "Certainly not a Fae-lover like you."

"She *is* a Fae-*lover* isn't she?" Scouvrel cooed, slipping in beside me to place two fingers intimately against my cheek.

I batted them away and shook my head, *tsking*. "Olen Chanter, you fool of a knight. If you don't realize by now that I'm the Fae's worst enemy, then you never will."

"Your sister ordered me beaten and tortured," Olen said through thick lips. "I don't even know what they did to Heldra." His voice broke. "To my children."

Good thing he couldn't see my sister in the cage on my belt or he'd really hate me right now. She snickered from the safety of her cage.

I cleared my throat awkwardly. "Well, if they went where I told them to go then they're all safe. Along with the other children from the town. And if any of you had listened to me in the first place, then Skundton wouldn't have been overrun by Fae armies and you wouldn't be captured. You could be serving the great Sir Eckelmeyer in the Queen Anabetha's court in the south."

"Sir Eckelmeyer lives," Olen said. "They sent him back to her – naked and painted yellow for cowardice."

Behind me, Scouvrel burst into laughter and it was all I could do not to join him. Really, Allie, it was a cruel thing to do. But why did the mental image of that pompous Eckelmeyer painted yellow seem so funny? I was a terrible, terrible person.

"Well, at least they didn't paint you," I said, pulling the golden key from my pack. I turned to Scouvrel and spoke with a sugary tone. "Husband of mine, could you spare a hair from your fine head?"

Olen's good eye looked like it might fall out of his head.

"In exchange for one secret," Scouvrel said slyly with a smile that promised it would be a painful thing for me. His eyes flickered constantly to the trees. We needed to hurry.

"It is agreed," I said, turning back to Olen. "We'll get you out of here, Sir Chanter, and then you can go find your Yellow Knight and take back Skundton from the Fae."

"I can't," Olen said. Despair was thick in his tone. "Even with the fights among our occupiers, they are still too strong. I'm like a child compared to them."

"Fights?" I asked absently as Scouvrel handed me his single hair with a dramatic flourish and bow. I accepted it and wrapped it around the key. That would be magic enough.

"Someone killed the Lord of the Court of Twilight during the fighting. I don't know who, but I'm grateful for that small mercy. It's why the army has stayed put for now. They're fighting to see who will succeed him."

Ooops.

That was my fault.

Olen snorted bitterly. "I'm surprised they don't just make whoever killed him take the role. I don't know half the time if the Fae fighting *want* to be the Lord or *don't* want to be the Lord."

"Probably both," I muttered, slotting the key into the lock.

"Trying to find a door won't help," Olen said to me. "I can see out of the cage, but I can't see it. I can feel it with my hands, but it feels wrong. It moves. It *hisses*."

"That's because it's made of snakes," I muttered as I turned the key.

Olen shuddered, his eyes rolling up. "Don't tell me that."

The door swung open and I jammed the key into my pocket.

"Here we go. Jump out."

He looked at me like I was crazy.

Scouvrel made an annoyed sound in the back of his throat and stepped past me, grabbing Olen by his neck and pulling him through the door of the cage.

"As much as it amuses me to watch you toy with this creature, we're wasting time, Nightmare. We need to move before the Courts realize you are here and come to take your power."

Olen stumbled and fell to the mossy forest floor. He scrambled to his feet, his eyes never leaving the spot beside Scouvrel.

"I'll never get used to not seeing them except when they want me to," he said, vibrating with something that felt like fury. "If the one you are calling your husband grabs me by the neck again ..."

His voice trailed off and he was left shaking his head as if he realized his threat was empty.

I grabbed Olen by the collar, pulling him close so I could look in his good eye with mine.

"Listen to me, Olen Chanter, because this is important. I'm fighting to stop this Fae invasion, but I can't do it alone. You're still the Knight in Skundton so it's time for you to rally the people, find allies, and fight for your town. You forgot everything about the Fae, but it's time to remember again. You told me the rhyme yourself: *Music to bind, Fire to blind, Look in their eye, With Iron they die.* Start playing music. Start lighting fires. Start finding the iron in your spine and in the land. We're going to need every ounce of it."

He nodded, quivering with both injured pride and agreement.

"Go," I said quietly, releasing his collar and jamming the axe handle into my belt. "I have my own things to attend to."

Something like a pair of hands seemed to be squeezing my throat. It was all I could do to draw my sword and slice the air before my vision flickered and I fell to my knees.

Chapter Seven

STRONG HANDS LIFTED me, stepped through the cut in the air and set me on a smooth floor. When I opened my eyes, I was in Scouvrel's secret hideaway – the one with all the books – staring directly at the bloodcurdling painting he'd made for me. The strange whorls and swirls of maroon on white twisted my stomach as I fought for breath.

A sudden – irrational – urge for violence filled me, rippling through me with images dancing across my vision of myself with bloody hands, slashing the throat of a person, of myself tying a noose, of myself twisting the handle of a knife into flesh. I retched, heaving as the images would not let up.

No, Allie, this is not you!

I was not needlessly violent. I did not take human life.

And yet, I could feel a desperate hunger tearing through me, trying to consume me with its intensity.

This was something beyond me.

"Don't fight it," I heard my sister's satisfied voice in the distance. "It will only kill you if you do. Accept your role. You are the Balance now. You bring order and governance to the Fae. You will serve as the hand of the High Queen of the Faewald."

Scouvrel growled something I couldn't make out and then the cage was snatched away from my belt. I reached toward it, but my eyes darkened with more visions. Worse, my blindfold was still over one of my eyes and the real world that I saw was so horrific and empty that I couldn't bear it. Where there were

45

high shelves of books and comfortable chairs in one eye's vision, the other saw nothing but a dark howling cave with shreds of something like torn fabric – or perhaps torn flesh – flapping in tatters from the walls.

I reached up and feebly tugged down my blindfold.

Enough. Enough of this nonsense.

Fighting the sensation, I stood, battling the queasy way my vision spun. I did not need to be ruled by this nausea or this – whatever this mental breakdown was.

Scouvrel stood in front of me, his face white.

"You confirm my fears, Nightmare. Despite your sweet rebellion, you will not withstand the Faewald."

"I'll withstand whatever comes for me," I said, gritting the words out between clenched teeth.

"Sweet Nightmare," he said, his face filled with heartbreak. "You feel it now. It is in your bones. You saved a human life. Now, you must take a human life."

"No," I said, and a pain like being stabbed by a knife plunged through my chest. I gasped, dropping back to one knee.

He was there immediately, drawing me close, clutching me like I was dying, his face torn. "Don't die now, Nightmare. I need you to do so much more. I need you to *be* so much more than this."

I tried to speak through clenched teeth, but the pain was too much.

"I'll make your bargain, Nightmare," he said through clenched teeth. "I will promise to keep fighting for you and not against you. Only please, stop fighting this. Don't die for my sake."

"I'm not fighting this for you," I said, each word a battle as the pain ripped through me.

"Then why fight it at all? Become the Nightmare you are. Fight me at every turn. Thwart all my plans. Be the Balance to my Rogue forever, Nightmare. We shall be locked in eternal combat and I shall welcome it for your sake. I will take every blow with pride and give every hurt with respect and we shall be grand and glorious adversaries forever!"

"I'm not killing anyone," I said all in a rush, pushing out of his embrace. "And I don't know why you'd want to bargain with me now when you wouldn't before. Didn't you listen to the frog I gave you? Didn't it tell you my name?"

He gave me a pitying look and paused before saying, "The frog remains silent as the graves of my enemies. Knowing your true name does nothing for me, horrible Nightmare. I have known it since your mother spoke it, and yet I cannot enchant you with it."

I grunted. I'd forgotten that.

"I think you'd better tell me why I feel like I'm dying," I said, my voice far weaker than I would like.

His hands hovered over me as if he was trying to figure out where to put them. "You cannot fight your role. I told you before that none of us can choose what role we play. We can only admit our parts in the play."

"Not good enough," I managed. Because it wasn't.

"It will kill you if you fight it."

"Give me your knife," I said.

His puzzled expression made me laugh despite the pain, but he slid a long, slender knife from his sleeve and handed it to me. The handle was carved with the head of a raven, the beak open in a squawk. I took it carefully and slit the end of a finger.

"Open up your hand," I said and when he did, I let the droplet fall into his hand. "Here's the secret you bargained for," I said through gritted teeth. "It's probably best that I pay it while I'm still alive to do it."

His eyes glittered, widening.

"The secret is this – I haven't decided to end our marriage yet and I'm not sure if I will. This drop of my blood is yours."

Maybe it was the pain. Maybe it was the extreme desire for violence that would not leave my heart – a desire that I knew could not originate with me – but the look on his face was not what I'd expected. I had expected curiosity or laughter. I had expected him to be pleased that I'd kept the bargain.

What I saw instead was absolute fury. It rippled over his face and he began to quiver as if a wave had washed over him, starting at the top of his head and quivering right down his body to his already-mostly-healed wounds and right down to his black boots.

"What have you done?" he snarled.

"I thought you'd like that," I said, surprised, my lips feeling thick as I tried to express myself despite my shock. "I thought you'd feel it was a worthy present to show that I appreciated your willingness to be my friend."

He leaned his face close to mine. "Are you so eager to end your life that you throw yourself at me like a used rag?"

"What?" I said, pushing him away. Something inside me was excited by his anger. Something that longed for violence. "What are you talking about? I just gave you what you want-ed!"

He shook his head and his body trembled with it as if every bit of him was denying me.

"You're tying me to you," he said. "You're desperate. It won't work."

He was kidding, right? He had to be kidding. He was the one who started this! He should be pleased that I was finally playing along!

"I'm not tying you to anything, you fool of a Fae!" I felt my lips trembling as my fury rose to match his. "Go, if that's what you want!"

And the minute I said those words all thoughts of violence fled. I could breathe again. I could think again. The pain was gone.

Balance.

I'd freed a human.

I'd freed a Fae.

He was gone before I could beg him to come back, leaving me in the room, shaking with emotion as my sister's laughter danced through the air.

Chapter Eight

"I WONDER HOW YOU'LL meet the last requirement if he isn't even around," my sister asked, taunting me as I ran to the door and snatched it open. In the piercing rays of dawn, the cloud layer below me was bright with pinks and soft peaches. Soaring between them, Scouvrel fell toward the earth. "You know you'll owe me something if you don't manage it. I think I'll take the current location of our parents as payment."

I slammed the door shut. I was stuck here. Other than using the sword, there was no way out.

I cursed.

"What's the final requirement?" I asked.

"You don't know?" She looked smug.

I grabbed her cage, carried it over to the small table and set it down there. Remains of the last meal Scouvrel fed me were still on the table – the cheese gone old and hard with mold over it and the nuts gone soft.

I grabbed a napkin from the table and stuffed it between the bars on Hulanna's cage.

"It's dawn. If you have nothing valuable to contribute then we should sleep while we can," I said miserably. My finger hurt. My heart hurt. And I didn't know what I'd done to make Scouvrel so angry. "I know I'm exhausted, and you probably are, too. Tomorrow, you're going to show me how to call back the Fae armies and end this war."

My sister laughed. "You must have quite the plan ready if you think you can talk me into that."

I ignored her, flopping down on the settee beside the table and closing my eyes. Sleep did not come easily. I tossed and turned. I wanted to yell at Scouvrel, to demand answers, to force him to listen. I almost wished I'd let those wings grow in my back so I could chase after him and force him to talk to me. The coward. He couldn't even face me like a man.

Eventually, my anger smoldered down to a dull haze and I drifted off to sleep.

I awoke with a sudden, sharp fear filling me.

The wagon.

If anyone stumbled on it, they would find my parents, the children – everyone. And the Fae were not far away from that wagon, even if they were in the middle of a succession war. I needed to go and deal with that. Immediately.

I jumped to my feet, gathered my things and looked out the door. It was noon. I still had time. Unless the trips to and from the Faewald played with time the way that they sometimes did.

I drew my sword and reached for Hulanna's cage.

"Mmmph, it's the middle of the day!" she grumbled. "No wonder you stayed human. You weren't born with a shred of decency. Rural trash."

I shook the cage. Her irritated squeal was as good as a morning cup of tea.

With a slash of the sword, the air split and I sheathed my sword and stepped out into the mortal world.

"We're going out somewhere? You didn't even give me time to bathe or water to drink!" Hulanna protested as I lifted the cage and tied it to my belt.

"I thought you didn't want to bargain, sister," I said as I slipped my blindfold up.

The magic of the sword was still working. The wagon was right in front of me, though it was late afternoon here already. I licked my lips, worried about the time jump. I couldn't afford days, weeks, or years lost. Every moment was precious right now.

"You've brought us to an old broken wagon. Your Court is so charming," my sister said acidly.

I ignored her and reached into my pack, drawing out the flint. I prepared a small nest of grass, drew my knife and began to lay a fire. I wanted to go through the door and to check – to be absolutely certain – that my mother and father had made it to safety along with Heldra and her children and all the others. I wanted it so badly it made me ache. But I didn't dare do that. The best way I could protect them right now was by staying away. The best way I could protect them was by making very sure that no one ever came looking.

I set the glowing nest against the base of the wagon and began to pile tinder against it.

"We were sisters," I said to Hulanna as I watched the fire build. "We were friends all our lives. We shared everything. Parents. Dresses. Food. Secrets. Everything."

"We didn't share dreams," she countered. "We didn't share aspirations. All you've ever wanted were this sorry old forest and the animals you kill like a savage. And I want more. I wanted it then and I want it now. I'd kill myself if I had to live like you. Like mother and father. Living in some moldy old house only big enough for one bedroom. Everything in it repaired and old. Grinding out a life without a single luxury. It's like hell. Your life is hell, Allie. I don't want it and I never have."

"Even if that means that you won't have us?" I asked. Which was stupid, stupid, stupid, Allie. Of course, she didn't want us. She'd nearly killed most of us. So why did I keep hoping that she'd change her mind? Why did I keep hoping to have my sister back?

"I just don't understand what's so hard for you to understand, Allie," Hulanna said. "It's you or me. Your version of reality or mine. Your sad, stilted future, or my glorious one. And I'm choosing me. I have to make my dreams a priority or they just won't happen. Is that really so hard for you to accept? You have what? Fifty years left as a human? And maybe you'll kill a few animals or if you're really lucky you'll have some babies and give them the same sorry future that you have. Well, I'm going to have centuries – maybe even millennia – as the ruler of the Faewald. I'll live a life of parties and laughter, of fashion and art, of fine foods and finer conversation, or intrigue, anticipation, wonder and magic. A life of power and prestige, of education and experimentation, and all earthly or Faewald delights. One life of mine won't just be ten times longer than yours would be. It will be a hundred times richer, a thousand times more valuable. It will be worth the sacrifice of ten-thousand mayfly lives like yours."

I didn't know what to say to that, as the flames licked up the side of the wagon, destroying the way to escape all this, removing the evidence, saving the people I loved best and trapping me here with the ones I needed to destroy.

I lifted the cage so that I could stare at her and imprint her image on my mind. I didn't want to ever forget what she'd just said or what she was willing to do.

Enough, Allie. Enough with believing the best about her. Enough thinking that blood was thicker than water. Enough.

Her flaw was cruelty.

My flaw was gullibility.

How did I expect to beat her if I kept playing into my flaw again and again?

She smirked at me and I let that sink in with the rest.

"Cat got your tongue?" she asked, lifting her brow. "Or is there just nothing you can say because you know I'm right?"

"You can't argue with evil," I said as the flames in the background swept up with a *whomp* and swallowed the wagon completely, a pillar of smoke swirling into the sky. "You can only extinguish it."

I'd hoped that maybe if the word "win" didn't mean capture then maybe it meant to persuade. But there would be no persuading Hulanna.

I didn't realize I was crying until I felt the sting in my eyes and cheeks. This was the end of my family. This was the end of my town.

But that wasn't who I was. I was Allie Hunter. I was this land. And there was iron seamed under the earth here in the heart of the mountains. Iron in the earth, iron in my blood, and iron in my will.

"You can't do anything without me," Hulanna said. "That's what the prophecy means. It's our curse. Stuck with each other until one of us is killed in the proper way."

"And which one do you think that will be?" I asked coldly as the wagon fell in on itself and the fire calmed.

It wouldn't be me. And now it wouldn't be the innocents I saved, either. I'd done that much, at least.

I waited until the sun had set and the fire had fallen to a low bed of ash before I pulled my sword from my sheath again and sliced through the air.

Chapter Nine

I SHOULD HAVE BEEN paying more attention to what I was wishing for when I slashed my sword through the air because I didn't come out anywhere that I recognized in the Faewald.

Hulanna's gasp came first and then my own right on her heels.

Kneeling on the ground, head bowed before us, was Scouvrel. He knelt before a towering set of doors that looked as if they were made of iron. The doors were set in a round frame – each a half-circle. The frame seemed to twist so that the eye refused to run along it properly. There was no wall or building the doors were set into. They just stood there as if they led nowhere – and yet that couldn't be true. Not with the faint screams I heard from behind the door.

Symbols I could not read and did not understand flowed in script over the door, intertwining with thorny vines, roses, wings, feathers, and owl eyes as they decorated the spaces between the grinning skeletons of Fae. Horns and long skeletal tails, skeletal scraps of wings and even a bony unicorn were clear indications that these were Fae shown here – but even more telling were the tangled, fraying edges of the Fae, waving out from them and tangling together like scraps of ragged flesh blown in a gale. Even in this spirit sight, the edges of the gate seemed to writhe and twist under my gaze.

I shuddered.

Heat pulsed from the door, searing hot so that my skin flushed immediately as if I were standing in front of the village forge. I swallowed as Scouvrel looked up, his eyes lighting with hope and his mouth dropping open.

"What are you doing at the Dread Doors?" Hulanna hissed from her cage. Eventually, she'd have to learn that she was the captive here.

"You're both here," he breathed, his eyes bright as if salvation had come to him. He stood slowly as the sun began to sink behind the hills and the shadows grew long and desperate. "Truth or lie? You came to me of your own free will."

"Truth," I said, slowly. What did he mean? Why did he look as though his life depended on my answer?

He whispered – as if he were talking to himself, debating something he'd argued with himself over a hundred times. "But who would ever choose to die for us?"

"No one would," Hulanna sneered. "Which is why you have to make her. Take her life right here on the Bloodstone, Knave. Take it while there is still time and you and I can rule together."

The stone under him really was red as if it had been soaked in generations of blood.

I still had the sword in my hand.

Something firmed in Scouvrel's expression. But whether that was because he was agreeing with her or denying her, I didn't dare to find out.

I slashed the sword and this time I thought of where I really wanted to be.

Nothing happened.

The last ray of light was gone.

A horn sounded in the distance, long and musical. The Wild Hunt was on. I needed to run.

I sheathed my sword, drawing my bow and an arrow instead.

"Don't touch me," I ordered Scouvrel, but my voice was faint.

I didn't understand what was happening here, but I didn't like this place. I needed to be gone – now.

I started to back away just as the horns sounded again. My eyes caught his and we shared a long look of confusion and desperation before I turned on my heels and began to run.

Feet pounded on the ground behind me. There weren't woods here, just rolling grassy fields and something rocky up ahead. I hoped the grass wasn't disguising gopher holes. One misstep and I could break an ankle.

I leapt with wide strides over anything resembling a hole in the ground. I wouldn't take chances.

Someone began to scream behind me. Wet snaps of jaws and snarls tore through the air. Sounds of a butcher shop and a rancid smell like behind the shop urged me to run faster.

Oddly, my sewn up back wasn't hurting me. In normal circumstances, I'd expect it to be in fiery pain.

I was getting close to the top of a rise. I pushed harder, my feet hitting the ground with bone-jarring thuds, each stride leaping through the air like a deer over a fallen log.

I cleared the rise and gasped. Below me, the rock had been hewn into a huge rocky bowl. Within it, working silently were hundreds of golems, their silhouettes bright scarlet in the rising Blood Moon.

They looked up at me as one.

I swallowed.

"What are they looking at?" I muttered.

"One of the four," Hulanna said snidely. "You don't even deserve the title. You certainly don't deserve to command golems."

Command? I could *command* this army of golems? I held my breath for a moment as the thought rocketed through my mind. It was exactly what I'd hoped for. I'd asked them why they didn't ride an army of golems into Skundton and take the place over. I'd been told it wrecked the game. Well, I wasn't playing a game. I felt a smile start to steal over my face.

"Though until you receive the full mantle of the Balance, I doubt you could get more than one at a time to listen to your mortal whims," my sister said.

"You're so helpful," I murmured, and she snorted cruelly.

But she had been helpful.

A snarl rippled through the air behind me and I gasped. The Wild Hunt was sprinting faster, pounding across the ground like a herd of caribou. The nearest of the hounds leapt toward me, drool flying from his jowls as he snapped at me. I shot an arrow toward him, but though it buried in his eye he didn't even pause, didn't even flinch.

I felt ill. I drew a second arrow, glancing back at the golem.

"To me!" I called to them. They stood still, paused in the mining I'd interrupted.

My sister laughed.

I let another arrow loose at the dog, but he was already too close, his open mouth swallowing the arrow as if it didn't exist, his jaws snapping at me.

"You can't kill what's dead already," my sister called to me.

"Like your heart?" I countered, jumping into the rock bowl and barely holding onto my balance as I half skidded, half fell down the loose shale toward the floor of the bowl.

I grabbed one of the golems as I passed, wrapping my arms around him to stabilize me from the fall. He froze and I looked up to his empty stone eyes. Around me, loose rocks fell and bounced, tumbling to form drifts around my feet.

"Can you hear me, golem?" I asked.

"Brilliant idea, Allie," my sister taunted. "Ask something without a voice to speak."

"I bid you to bear me on your shoulders and run from the Wild Hunt," I said to the golem. "Will you agree to this?"

The golem said nothing.

I cursed quietly under my breath as the wild hound leapt over the edge of the bowl, flying through the air with all the doggy delight of a mortal hound jumping into a pond. I clenched my jaw, bracing for impact.

Smooth stone arms seized me, flinging me up onto a wide shoulder. I grunted in pain as I hit the shoulder with my tail-bone. The cage clanged with the sound of metal on rock and my sister's curses filled the darkening air.

I reached to my belt and grabbed my torch, lifting it into the air. Spirit light stained the world around us as the golem ducked away from the hound. The beast landed, nose to the ground, searching.

We'd be invisible, but I couldn't cloak our scent.

"Run," I breathed, my eyes refused to be torn from the slathering hound. His incisors were as long as my hands. His powerful musk filled my nose with dread.

The golem lurched forward, slowly gaining speed – step by ponderous step. But nothing can stop a creature made of rock once it gets momentum. Small rocks bounced easily off his heavy legs and as we crested the edge of the bowl and out onto the plains again, long grasses and tangling vines snapped and fell in a swath behind him. He was glorious and steady – faster than I was on foot – and yet utterly silent. With the torch held high, I watched for the chase.

"Smart move. The dogs won't smell golem. They're just rocks," my sister said.

A loud baying cut the air and the hounds leapt again. On one of them, the terrifying man with the ram's horns and whip-like braid seemed to pause, staring at me for a half a moment before throwing back his head and laughing.

My heart jumped into my throat. But when they sprinted away, it was in the other direction. They had other quarry to hunt.

I breathed a sigh of relief, swung my leg around so I could sit straddling both the golem's shoulders, and held my torch high. I didn't know where we would find shelter, but until we did, we had to stay on the alert. The Wild Hunt was a'hunting and Allie Hunter was no prey.

Chapter Ten

WE DASHED THROUGH THE landscape to where grass morphed to shrubs and shrubs to huge mushrooms and huge mushrooms to trees. In the span of moments, we were under a canopy of spreading birches, the golem silent as he strode with the smooth efficiency of something made of magic and rocks.

I dared to breathe a sigh of relief.

Too soon.

Behind me, the baying began again, the hounds of the Wild Hunt chasing after us.

"Hurry," I gasped as the trees rushed by – stripes of delicate white against a dark sultry sky.

We were deep into the woods where the trees were growing taller and wider and thinning out to where we could walk easily under their spreading branches, their trembling leaves making shadows shiver through the red moonlight on the forest floor. A clearing spread out before us - in its center an ethereal spire rose, gleaming and bright as it shot toward the heavens. It made my mind sing a note as if someone had run his damp finger around the rim of a glass.

I gasped.

But while I was still fixated on the spire, movement sprang into my line of vision.

A hound!

They'd lulled us into a sense of safety, and then driven us forward into a trap. They must have known this spire was here.

Two of them sprang from the trees to join the first. I could almost see their wicked grins under the snap of their teeth.

"Now you've killed us both," Hulanna said. "Still feeling clever?"

One of the hounds leapt toward us, a ball of muscle and slather and snarling, snapping cries. Our golem dodged to the side, but my weight made him awkward. The hound barely missed us, turning in mid-air to spin back toward us, the bright blood of the moon painting his edges in red and white.

The single reverberating note from the spire – still ringing in my mind – made it hard to think. My heart pounded with it, frightened. Racing.

What now? The other two hounds stalked toward us, their eyes gleaming as they kept us pinned in place for their pack member to make the kill. And behind them, I began to hear tinkling laughter as Fae mounted on stags and owlgriffins, pangolins, and phoenixes hurried to join them in their hunt – a flurry of magic and malformed creatures twisted by this place into ghoulish killers.

A hound emerged on the horizon and on its back – silhouetted by the Blood Moon – was a hulking black figure. His tail swished impatiently in the moonlight. He smiled slowly, surely, certain of his kill. He reached behind him and drew a short spear from his back, hefting it in a palm as he looked at me – judging the distance.

"Fool of a sister. Waste of breath!" My sister cursed at me.

But I wasn't done yet. I had forgotten something in all this magic and all this glamor. I had forgotten that I was mortal. And as a mortal, I had a gift they didn't have.

I began to sing.

"I sing of my love, of my mountain lad,
A tale of a love both warm and sad."

I'd never been much of a singer – I was horribly off-key – but it didn't seem to matter.

"Of brooks of laughter and tangled song,
Of summer days mellow, soft, and long."

My sister froze first in her cage. A hound lunged toward us and froze mid-snap.

"A love I lost through a fool mistake,
A heart that suffers from endless break."

My song rippled outward, and every Fae that heard a note drew up abruptly and listened. Except for the golem.

"I sing of soft promises under the star,
The sting of their lies still can't mar."

We strode through their frozen shapes, and I noted every cruel twist to a mouth, every glistening blade, red in the moon, every exposed tooth – sharp and deadly. There were no kind souls here – only the vengeful. Only those banned from an afterlife to chase after the Fae and drag them to the depths. I shivered, but I didn't stop my song.

"The love of a boy who loved me not,
Who triumphed only that I was caught."

We ran past the press of the frozen hunt – their still silhouette's snatching my breath away. Their faces were twisted in cruel expressions, their eyes full of hate and they quivered in their frozen forms as if trying to break the spell. Through the forest, I sang the song over and over again until I thought my lungs would burst of it. Why had I not done this before?

"Who delighted to know I was in his hand,
Whose affection was smaller than grains of sand."

Until we came to a bubbling stream. Beside it, on tall legs carved to look like the feet of birds, with a strange sharp-angled roof that looked like black wings tucked around it, was a small cottage. A streak of mud was slashed across the door. Earth-marked.

I tapped the golem on the shoulder, pointing to the cottage while I sang.

"He left me broken and half a girl,
He left my heart in a deadly swirl."

We opened the door and stepped into a tangled cottage so full of trinkets and knickknacks, of decorations and stuffed creatures, of twinkling will-o-the-wisps caught in lanterns – that it took me a full breath to even determine if anyone else was there. The cottage was empty of living Fae, though not of many dead taxidermized animals and ... I hoped that wasn't a person.

"And never will I ever love again,
Or think of the charms of my mountain man."

I slipped down from the golem's shoulders and closed the door behind me, barring it with care.

"Ah, but maybe he did love you. Maybe he loved you so deeply that the word itself was meaningless."

I startled at Scouvrel's voice, spinning to look for him. He loomed in a full-length mirror half-draped with a colorful dressing robe. I yanked the robe aside.

"You've found safety, Nightmare," he said with a smile.

"Truth or lie," I said with a quavering voice. "You almost killed me back at that door."

He regarded me for far too long with his smoldering gaze. A muscle in his jaw jumping as he tensed and untensed it.

He swallowed before he finally spoke in a bold tone as if to dare me to stop him.

"Truth. But not for the reason you think."

I set my sister's cage on a stack of eggs – empty, I hoped – and threw the dressing gown over it. She was still frozen within, even though my song had stopped. As soon as I was sure she couldn't hear me, I stepped to the mirror and gave Scouvrel a piercing look.

"Let me be very clear, Knave," I said. "Killing me – for any reason at all – is not welcome."

"Let me be very clear, Nightmare," he said with a teasing smirk. "Your death would hollow me, empty me, destroy whatever flickering ember of a soul I ever had and doom me to eternal torment."

I gasped. He couldn't lie. So how could he say these things to me?

"Then why seek my death?" I asked, bringing my hand up to touch the mirror despite myself. My voice was more vulnerable than I wished it would be.

He winked and put his own hand up to touch mine as if he could reach it through the glass.

"I do not seek it. I offer it. And hope it will be enough."

I shivered. "This has to end. You have to stop pretending that you're obsessed with me, that you are on my side ... that you admire me on the one hand while on the other hand, you keep vowing to kill me and then almost doing it. Eventually, one of us really will kill the other." I cleared my throat, forcing aside my sudden turbulent fears. "And it will be me killing you, Scouvrel. Make no mistake about that. I am better at killing than you are. I am braver and stronger and just plain *better*."

His smile grew affectionate as I spoke. "And that, my elusive Pursuit, is what I would pray for if I was audacious enough to pray. It is what I would wish for, if I were foolish enough to wish. It is what I would long for if I were not a shriveled empty husk beyond longings."

I snorted. "Then just *stop!* Stop turning against me and work with me. I even gave you my blood. That means I only need to do one more thing to complete my marriage to you. If that isn't a promise that we can be allies, then what is? Stop fighting me and be on my side!"

He licked his lips as if he were considering it, snagging the edge of his lip between his teeth in a far-too-seductive fashion.

"Truth or lie?" he asked. "You don't know what the fourth thing is."

I scowled and he laughed.

"It will be a delight to trick you into it, then."

"But I am forewarned. You will trick me into nothing." I narrowed my eyes.

He sobered. And that terrified me.

"Truth or lie?" I said, trying not to let my voice tremble. "You won't stop trying to kill me. Not even if I finish confirming our marriage."

He leaned his forehead against the mirror on his side and I leaned mine against the cold glass on my side, wishing I could step through it to him and actually feel his chest heaving as it was doing right now, that I could smooth away the turmoil on his face until he denied what I just said, until he admitted that he liked me far too much to kill me.

"Truth," he gasped.

I recoiled, tears stinging my eyes.

Silly Allie, silly. To think that the monster could become anything else. To think that you – of all people – could inspire that. What a terrible fool I was.

I felt a single hot tear sear down my cheek.

"Then the next time I see you," I said coldly, feeling my features harden. "I will be forced to slay you."

"May I not have a last meal?" he drawled. "Even executioners allow that."

"What?" I had just told him I was going to kill him and he asked for *food*?

"Let me feast on your kisses one more time. Let me sate myself on your hot wrath and fevered gaze."

I rolled my eyes. "I am serious, Scouvrel."

He looked almost breathless as his other hand reached up to press against the glass, too, fingers splayed wide.

"As am I."

"Then you should know that I won't die easily. And I will kill you with solid iron before you get the chance to kill me," I said, drawing the sword from my belt.

I smashed the mirror before he could reply. He was all seductive charm and alluring promises.

I didn't dare believe any of them.

Though, like the girl in the song, I feared I would never love again. He'd ruined me for that.

Chapter Eleven

"AND NOW," I SAID, RIPPING the dressing gown from my sister's cage. "We have to deal with things here."

"What things?" Hulanna asked with a smirk. "Threatening your husband? It was nicely done, but to be honest, I found a surprise attack worked best."

"So I saw," I said dryly. "But that is not what I'm talking about. I am referring to how I will reward this golem for his help."

I turned to the hulking rock sculpture. It seemed impossible for him to have an expression, but more than anything else, he looked surprised.

"It's a *golem*. It doesn't get rewards," my sister said.

"You're the Lady of Cups," I said coolly, never taking my eyes off the golem. "A few days ago, you wouldn't have expected to be caged like a pet bird. But here we are. A golem can have a reward. Just like you can be caged."

I could feel the rightness of that in my bones as my eyes watched the golem's marble eyes.

"You don't have the magic to give him anything," my sister said. "Nor the wealth nor the power."

But I did have magic. I could feel it crackling at my fingertips. The feeling took my breath away. I had it if I used it the right way. And that meant balance.

I squinted my eyes and tried to think.

He'd given me his service of his own free will tonight. A gift for a gift. That was balance, wasn't it?

"He can't even tell you what he wants," my sister said. "You're wasting your time."

"Then maybe he should be able to do that," I said quietly, guided by a tugging in my belly. And just like that, the spark of magic was gone, the singing sound of a finger on a glass had disappeared from my mind and I was just Allie again. I met the golem's eyes with chagrin. "Sorry to get your hopes up. I thought I could give you a voice."

"SO DID I," he boomed. It sounded strange from his expressionless stone face.

"Oh, well then," I said surprised. "Ummm, are you hungry?"

I looked around frantically, but there didn't seem to be anything to eat.

"Stars and skies, Allie!" my sister cursed. "He's a *golem*. He's made of *rock.*"

"I DO NOT REQUIRE FOOD. REVENGE MIGHT BE NICE."

"I don't think there will be any revenge tonight," I said drily as his gaze drifted to my sister. I pulled a waterskin out of my pack and filled the thimble I had left with it. I was getting used to keeping prisoners. "Here."

I offered the thimble to my sister and took a long drink of my own before replacing my waterskin in the pack. I needed sleep. I'd only had a few hours before. And we were safe here in this house for now.

"What's your name?" I asked the golem.

"I HAVE NO NAME," he said.

"I think I'll call you Rocky, if that doesn't bother you. It will be easy to remember."

"EASE IN REMEMBERING IS PRAGMATIC."

"You are naming a golem," my sister said rolling her eyes. "It's as pathetic as naming the bunnies we used to have as children. They were just going to be soup in the winter. You always knew that but you always had to name them."

"I'm going to sleep," I announced. "But not in that bed. The rest of you can do what you want."

Eventually, I settled for sleeping with my back against the door. Rocky, to my great surprise, took the bed, his feet hanging off the end from the knees down. I hadn't even realized that golems could sleep. Maybe they couldn't. Maybe he was just enjoying the fact that he had the option.

I fell asleep imagining what it would be like to have a name for the first time in your life.

It was light when I awoke to something hitting me on the face. I scrambled to my feet, heart in my throat, hand on my bow, but my sister's wry laughter was the only threat. She'd thrown a bead at me. It rolled across the floor and landed in a pile of ribbons under the table.

"Something wicked this way comes," she whispered.

If she thought she was getting out of that cage, she was wrong.

I wiped a hand across my eyes. What now? I had the golem as an ally. I had my sister. What I needed was a way to get her to stop her people, and an army to quell them. I shied away from what I realized yesterday – that the prophecy demanded that one of us "win" the other and that I'd discovered that could only mean "kill." I wasn't ready to think about killing my sister.

No – it was more than not being ready. I wasn't *going* to kill my sister. There were some lines you just shouldn't cross.

"Do you think your golem friends would be willing to help me, Rocky?" I asked at the same time that something hit the door of the little cottage. It shook, the smaller items falling from their shelves and piles and a cloud of dust filling the air.

I snatched my sister's cage from the pile of eggs at the same time that several of them fell to the floor, cracking to tiny pieces, revealing nothing but colored dust inside. The dust rose into the air like litte columns of smoke, filling the air with a variety of scents both sweet and putrid, from the scent of rotting fungus to the scent of gardenias.

I tied her cage to my belt hurriedly, coughing at the choking scents.

"So eager to escape your destiny?" she teased. "I don't think you'll shake him so easily. He knows what he wants."

"Who knows what they want?" I asked, my breath coming quicker as I fumbled the knot.

Slow down, Allie. Be calm.

I got it the second time.

"Your nemesis," my sister said. "The one who must take your life according to prophecy."

"I thought that was you," I said.

My hand shook as I drew the sword from the scabbard. It rattled noisily on the way out.

"Coming, Rocky?" I asked as I sliced the sword through the air.

The door behind me shattered, swinging inward with the power of the next blow against it. My eyes widened as I spun to see a cloud of dust and debris filling the entrance to the cabin. My heart was pounding so hard I saw red with every beat.

"If you're coming, you need to go through first," I said.

No answer from the golem.

From the clouds of settling dust, a dark figure emerged, his eyes – wrathful and huge – held mine like a serpent's might hold a mouse.

"You're avoiding me," my husband said through clenched teeth.

I stepped through the tear in the air, calling behind me, "And I'm doing it very well!"

I stumbled so hard on the other side that I fell to my knees, almost impaling myself with the rusty sword as my sister laughed delightedly.

"This is fun," she purred. "Like watching one of my romance novels in the flesh. Oh, the drama! Oh, the torment! Oh, the unrequited love! But this story will only end in tragedy and I prefer the ones with the happy endings."

"Like the one where you killed your espoused?" I asked, but I wasn't paying attention as I tried to slide the sword into the sheath, my spirit vision dull and dark in the mortal world.

"Oh, I haven't killed her yet," a voice said, and I froze.

Chapter Twelve

A HAND SEIZED THE BACK of my neck and I spun, twisting against it, trying to get my sword up. I was flung back. I fell, my head smacking against the ground. I rolled, coming up on my feet, my heart pounding, my breath racing.

I'd lost the sword. I couldn't see very clearly, though the old, twisting man in my spirit vision was horribly familiar.

Sir Eckelmeyer.

"I'm not your wife," I said, reaching for my bow and arrows. My reaching hand was grabbed and shoved behind me roughly. I bit back a cry.

Hands grabbed my other arm before I could reach for my dagger.

My sister snickered in her cage, unheard and unseen by the mortals who had captured me. On either side of me, the wavering spirits of mortal soldiers sprang to life, their unraveling ends twisting and writhing in the spirit darkness. I thought longingly of the torch in my belt and of the sword on the ground. Either one would help me – if only I could reach them.

I shoved against the man on my left, but I couldn't budge his grip. He was twice my size, and even in the spirit world his arms were the girth of my thighs.

"Bring her with us. The Queen will settle on what to do with my wife."

"I told you," I said, "I'm not your wife."

His strike came too fast for me to see with my spirit vision. My vision darkened as the pain shot through my face, leaving me spitting blood. My teeth had torn the inside of my mouth. Pain flared through my nose and across my cheekbones – a dull throbbing pain that made me grit my teeth. Was it broken?

I snarled. I wasn't easy prey – despite my current circumstances. And I certainly was no wife to him.

"I married you in absentia when you disappeared from Sir Chanter's cellar," Sir Eckelemeyer said. "And even though you practice the black arts and are the friend of the Fae, I will see you turned back to the right."

"Let me guess," I said through my swelling lip. "Turning me back to the right involves an enormous amount of pain on my part, ending in certain death."

"Well, you might be evil, wife," he said mildly, "but at least you are not stupid."

"Fae forfend," I mocked.

Something seized my hair, pulling it almost out by its roots and I was shaken like a kitten in a large dog's mouth.

"No talk like that when we see the Queen, or your death will be more painful than you already imagine."

It wasn't hard to see why Sir Eckelmeyer had found such difficulty in procuring a wife. It took force, threats, and certain death to bring a woman to him.

"Is that a fleck of yellow paint I see on your ear?" I asked through clenched teeth.

His hand rose just a hair and then his eyes narrowed and another blow filled my head with darkness. I blinked against the agony, gasping for breath and coughing on the blood trickling down the back of my throat.

"How do you feel about that as a punishment for your defiance, wife?"

"Delightful mortal," my sister said from her cage. "Who would have thought that you, Allie. You! Would be so popular that more than one man married you against your will. It's almost like a story."

"I'm thrilled," I muttered to her through thick lips.

"Good," Sir Ecklemeyer said, thinking I was addressing him. "You should be. It is the highest of honors to come before Queen Anabetha herself."

They marched me between what looked like tents – though the encampment was hard to see in my spirit vision. Inanimate objects didn't make much impression in the spirit world. The place could be full of all manner of worldly goods from barrels to crates to armaments to attire and my spirit vision would only see the dullest of hints. Even with slight, barely-there views around me, I thought I was seeing dozens and dozens of matching tents. The fires and the soldiers around them were easier to see. The men came in every form from bright and shining with noble visages to utterly bent and shriveled, their edges unwinding or almost completely unwound – like Sir Eckelmeyer.

That was mortals for you. They came in every shade of morality. And that made it so difficult to know what to do with them. How did you slaughter them knowing there were a few noble and bright among them? How did you refrain knowing there were just as many dark and twisted?

I shook my head. I was avoiding the real problem.

How was I going to escape? I hadn't fled Scouvrel just to end up imprisoned by someone worse.

And what was I going to do once I did escape? The golem army was a good idea, but I'd lost my golem friend. Capturing my sister was a good idea, but she wasn't open to stopping the invasion of the mortal world and I wasn't open to killing her. Besides, the Wild Hunt was still going and Scouvrel – for whatever reason – was still trying to kill me.

I seemed to inspire murderous violence in anyone calling himself my husband.

We passed through masses of people, the soldiers pushing me in front of them with no concern for whether I tripped or was injured along the way. I fell twice, the soldiers' grips on my arms twisting them painfully when I fell.

"I can see why you've failed so spectacularly in stopping us," my sister said from her cage. "You can't even seem to get along with your own allies."

On the top of a knoll, someone had built a structure like an open town hall. It had a roof, but the sides were open and a wide deck had been laid out around it. Even with only hints from my spirit vision, I could tell it was quickly constructed.

As we neared it, a few dozen horses rode up, the leader throwing up his hand to halt them when he saw Sir Eckelmeyer.

"Back so soon, Chanter?" Eckelmeyer asked.

It took me a moment to realize that it was Olen on the back of the horse. My breath sucked away.

"He's getting worse," my sister cooed delightedly. "How much time do you think has passed here to see him unravel so?"

He was unraveling. While his chin and shoulders slumped, his edges were swirling in the breeze and flapping behind him like flags. He was slowly, certainly, unspooling.

"We quelled their attack on the east ridge," Olen said, but his horrifying gaze seemed to be on me as he spoke. "We had to light fires this time to push them back. Music alone was not enough. Somehow, they have ways to counter it."

Then how had it been so effective on the Wild Hunt? Was it possible that music had more power over the Fae *inside* the Faewald?

"I've been telling you from the start that it was only a delaying tactic, brother," Eckelmeyer said. "At least we have a key to greater success now. My wife has returned."

Olen said nothing to that, simply watching me.

"He hasn't changed one bit," my sister said. "Even now, as a great and powerful knight here to protect his people – even now he has no spine. Isn't that interesting? People never really change. They can't. They're set from birth down a feeble path or a great one. I find it expedient to eliminate those on the feeble path."

There was a lot I wanted to say to that. And no way I was going to say it in front of Olen and Sir Eckelmeyer.

I kept my tongue silent as Eckelmeyer pulled me forward.

"Sir Hastings arrives tonight with one hundred crossbows," he told Olen. "He's been marching double-time since Rowland and he's to arrive tonight. After that, no more delays. No more mitigations. We'll attack in full force and crush them utterly."

"For Queen Anabetha," Olen said, but he sounded more resigned than enthusiastic.

I grunted as Eckelmeyer grabbed my blindfold and pulled me up the steps by it.

"Not a word out of you when we stand before the Queen," he muttered as another column of men marched in loudly from the south. Cries of greeting rang out and cheers. "You'll speak when spoken to, stay on your knees, and pray to whatever Fae you worship that we don't decide to take your treachery out on your family."

"And who would that be?" I taunted. "You? You are my husband after all – in absentia."

He hissed, but we were too close now for him to dress me down. We crested the height of the platform and before I could get a good look at the people assembled there, he shoved me to my knees, forcing my head down with his hand until it touched the rough-hewn wood.

"Your Glorious Majesty, Lady of the Morning, Bright Star of the Heavens," he announced. "It is my great privilege to offer to you a piece of my property to make use of as you so please – my prodigal wife has returned."

"After six months?" the Queen said. "How charming."

Six months? My breath caught in my throat. I'd lost time again. And time was something I didn't have.

Chapter Thirteen

IN THE CAGE STILL TIED to my belt, my sister laughed. "Not so certain of yourself now, are you sister? Imagine what you've probably missed these past six months."

"Stand her up, Eckelmeyer. One wishes to see your blushing bride."

I was jerked upward by my braid and I struggled to get my feet under me.

"Why is she loaded up like a pack mule? Remove all that fiddle-faddle."

The soldiers began to strip off my pack, bow, axe handle, and scabbard as I took in the queen.

We had always spoken of the faraway queen who claimed Skundton as part of her territory but until now I'd never met anyone from my town who'd actually seen her. Even her tax collectors didn't come so far up into the mountains.

And yet, here was the queen in the flesh.

She wore a dress with a skirt so wide that it was impossible for anyone to get too close to her. Clever. It's much harder to slide a dagger secretly between someone's ribs if you can't get within four feet of her. Her skirts were stiff as wood and just as unyielding. And a thick, stiff collar ringed her head, protecting her neck the same way that stiff shoulder-guards capped her shoulders and ran along the tops of them to meet the collar. Though caps and collar all looked like they were made of white lace, they were so stiff that I suspected they were made of metal instead. Very clever. She wore armor without seeming to. Even her bodice was sharp and straight and unyielding. More armor. Her sleeves extended to points out past her longest finger. If I were designing a dress for a queen, this is what I would design – complete with the crown that was more a steel cap than anything else. The cabochon rubies ringing it did not fool me for a second. This finery was designed against attack.

The soldiers finished stripping me of my magical goods, reaching finally for the cage.

"If it please you, your Gracious Majesty," I said but I had to stop when Eckelmeyer cuffed me across the face again. The pain in my nose and lip flared hot again, flooding my mind with stabs of agony. Was it any wonder that he remained unmarried until he stole me as a bride?

"I believe she was speaking to me and not to you, Adam," the queen said to Eckelmeyer.

Adam? His first name was *Adam*. Not Vincent or Edward or Gladius but something as simple as ... Adam?

He saluted sharply. "Yes, Your Glorious Majesty."

I met her eyes for the first time. In the spirit world, people's true nature was shown in their eyes. I gasped as I realized that what I was seeing – in all her foxy glory, the queen was a Fae woman.

I gasped.

From in the cage, my sister snickered.

"Mortal is as mortal does, and this Queen of this little Court is no mortal at all. I wonder how she has managed to rule here so long unbeknownst to us."

The queen's left eye twitched at that, but she did not so much as glance toward my sister in her cage. Her blue eyes brightened as she looked at me and her hair – golden even in my spirit vision – surrounded her doll-like face like the corona of a saint.

"So, this is the lover of the Fae. Come closer, child. Show me your true loyalty."

I was shoved toward her down a line of courtiers or generals or something. In my spirit vision, they were so tangled, frayed, or hunched that it was hard to discern what they were in the human world.

"Bring her trinkets with her," the queen added as if by afterthought. But I knew the truth. She wanted my sister, too. And if she really was Fae – and there was no doubt in my mind that she was, then she knew what she could do with the two of us.

"Don't think to threaten me, quisling," my sister hissed as the guards carried her forward. "Even from this cage, I have the power to level you like a housewife pounding rising bread."

That left eye twitched again. The queen should really watch that tell. She told the whole world what she was thinking when she did that.

"That's close enough, Sir Eckelmeyer," the Queen said and Eckelmeyer forced me to the ground again. "Give her the cage she brought. Hold it up so I can see what you have there, child."

"Don't say a word, Allie," my sister hissed. "You don't know who you're talking to."

The queen winked at us as I lifted the cage up. But now that it was in my hands, an inspiration rocketed through me, lightning-fast. I started to smile.

"What a fine wife you've chosen, Sir Eckelmeyer. One is pleased to see you have thought of your nation before all else," the Queen said.

"She's not human," my sister said. As if I couldn't tell that already. "She's a changeling. But worse. A Changeling would fight for her people." She didn't mean that the fae had stolen a child and left her in that child's place ... did she? I'd heard a story like that but never given it credit. "This one has chosen to turn against us. Just as I want to conquer the mortal lands, she wants to conquer the Faewald. You think that by siding with her you can prevent war? Think again. I know Malentric. I know her ways. I have heard the stories of how she was switched for a sixteen-year-old princess. How the girl who had once been Anabetha was killed slowly, her blood poured over the bloodstone to seal the stone circle open and to give Malentric the perfect impenetrable glamor."

"What shall we do with your prize, Sir Eckelmeyer?" the Queen asked. "Shall we put a collar around her neck with a long chain and have her lead us to her Faerie allies?"

"That is precisely what I had hoped, Glorious Majesty," Sir Eckelmeyer said. I didn't need to look up to see the gleam in his eyes.

"If I wasn't in this cage," Hulanna said. "I would rip her limb from limb."

"I dare you to try," I said to all of them at once.

The Queen's eyes narrowed with rage, but my smile only grew. What I was about to do was her own fault. She shouldn't have let me have my cage back.

I looked at her armored, crowned figure and I thought of her as small.

She disappeared.

Around me, the crowd gasped, scrambling backward in a flurry of sudden movement as if they could escape a similar fate.

In the cage, a piercing scream rang out and the clang of something hitting the metal bars.

I didn't have time to see who was screaming.

"She's a witch!" Eckelmeyer roared and then everything went black.

Chapter Fourteen

I AWOKE TO THE SMELL of flames and rippling agony of pain flooding through me.

My eyes snapped open. The last thing I'd heard was the word "witch" and if they thought they were going to burn me, they could think again!

In front of me, Eckelmeyer was heating something over a flame. His spirit form twisted over hunched shoulders as he moved the glowing brand in the coals.

Curses filled my mind. That was for me. I just knew it.

My head hurt. I tried to touch my forehead, but my arms were lashed to a pole behind me, stretched wide. My feet, likewise, were lashed wide apart and my shoulders and waist tied, too.

I would be a spectacle.

Below me, I could see a crowd had formed, their spirit selves flickering and glowing, bright and then dark, whole and then fraying. Anticipation swirled through them dark as molasses and just as thick as it ebbed and flowed.

I bit back a panicked whine. No time to panic, Allie. Think!

But it was so hard to think with my heart beating so fast and my breath hitching in my throat.

I couldn't capture Eckelmeyer in the cage. I wasn't holding it. I couldn't even see it – or any of my things.

"Awake, wife?" Eckelmeyer asked from beside the fire. "Then you are ready. I am going to brand you as a traitor. And then you will tell us how to get Queen Anabetha the Pure and Noble back from your dark magic spell."

A string of curses paraded through my mind. I couldn't think. I couldn't plan.

The brand lifted from the fire – a bright upside-down crown.

My heart sped up, beating so fast that I couldn't calm it. My breath soaring with it, faster, faster, faster. He was going to brand me. It was going to be agonizing. I wasn't ready.

"Where shall we put the mark?" Eckelemeyer crowed to the crowd.

Various answers called out to him and none of them sounded good. He turned to them, lifting the glowing brand high above his head as they cheered.

"The cheek? Did I hear the cheek?" he encouraged them. "The forehead?"

My stomach turned. My vision was swirling. I couldn't breathe.

"Cheek!" I heard the roar.

"Left or right?" he bellowed, clearly enjoying his depravity.

I clenched my teeth tightly, but I couldn't prevent the whine of fear from escaping them or the heave of my stomach. I was going to be ill.

There was a sound like an eagle descending, of wings catching the air. My hair blew back from my face.

And then a bright figure landed on the platform between Sir Eckelmeyer and me, his smoky wings swirling in black, flickering pillars. I knew those velvety wings. The bright figure snatched the brand from Eckelmeyer's hand – I knew that muscular form. But it was impossible. How could he have found me? And why was he saving me when he swore to kill me himself?

Eckelmeyer spun, snatching a dagger from his waist as his lips curled in a grimace of anger. He swung at Scouvrel who ducked under the swipe with a laugh. I felt my own laugh of relief bubble up from my horrified lips.

The Knave was fast, his movements liquid and flowing. He slid under Eckelmeyer's reach, spinning to pop up behind him, grabbed Eckelmeyer's hair with his right hand and shoved him forward so quickly that the knight fell to his knees. Scouvrel shoved Eckelmeyer's head even further down, his jacket tearing down the back at the force of his movements, until Eckelmeyer's forehead touched the wooden platform. Lightning fast, he jammed the blazing brand to Eckelmeyer's hip, letting it sear through his breeches as he howled.

Something squeaked. That wasn't me, was it?

"Left, I think," Scouvrel said coolly, throwing the brand into the crowd. His features in my spirit vision were the feral, foxy features of the Fae in this world – his clothing dirty scraps and his face gaunt and harrowed. Wicked delight lit his features.

There was a cry as people dodged the flying brand, falling over each other to get away.

Eckelmeyer moaned, struggling to his feet. But he'd been knighted for a reason. His sword was free of his scabbard and with only a small limp as evidence of what must be agonizing pain, he thrust his sword at Scouvrel. Scouvrel's brass needle was out of the scabbard before I could blink. He flicked the thrust away as Eckelmeyer cursed at the knights below.

"Don't interfere! I'll take the Fae down myself!"

Scouvrel's blade plunged toward him, but as Eckelmeyer's rose to defend, Scouvrel's plunged suddenly, darting to his knee. Blood blossomed from Eckelmeyer's breeches.

"Don't lose heart, Sir Knight," Scouvrel said. "I've been playing with swords since before you were out of wet naps. Wait. Was that only last year? I think that's what your mother told me when I saw her last."

"Don't talk about my mother," Eckelmeyer said, dancing back from Scouvrel's darting attack. "You have too much interest in my women. Why are you interfering with the punishment of my wife?"

"Wife?" Scouvrel asked and a spark of fury leapt into his eyes. "I fear, Knight, that if you use your tongue for such demonic lies, I shall have to pluck it out from your head and feed it to the eagle watching us from yon tree."

He flicked his blade for emphasis.

"She was given to me by her town and their elders confirmed our marriage in absentia," Eckelmeyer declared. "Which means she is legally mine to punish as I will."

"Is she?" Scouvrel hissed, leaning in so fast that I gasped. He was past Eckelmeyer's guard while my jaw was still falling open, in so close that I thought he might kiss the other man. Instead, he leaned in – light as a bird – and with a snap of his jaws like the beak of an eagle, he bit.

Eckelmeyer screamed as Scouvrel jumped back, spitting something from his mouth.

"Name this mortal 'wife' again and next time it will be worse than your ear," he said as Eckelmeyer's hand clamped over his ear, blood pouring down his neck. The look of shock on his face mirrored mine as Scouvrel lifted a leg lazily, planted the foot on Eckelmeyer's chest and pushed, sending him over the side of the platform.

Chapter Fifteen

AND THEN MY FAE HUSBAND was there, wiping blood from his chin with his sleeve and cutting my bonds with a small silver knife. He snatched me up to toss over one shoulder.

"I thought Fae couldn't fly in the mortal world," I said, too shocked to know what else to say.

"Well, not for long," he agreed. "But I didn't need to fly for long. ROCKY!"

The golem lumbered through the crowd, flinging people out of his way. I gasped. Those were humans! That wasn't ... well, I could hardly say it wasn't right after what they were about to do to me, could I?

I focused on something with less moral ambiguity.

"You bit his ear off!"

"Now your two husbands match. I thought you'd like the symmetry of that, Balance."

Rocky reached us at the same moment that I heard a rallying cry from the soldiers around us.

"Defend the Queen!"

Strange cry for a group whose queen was missing.

The golem reached down and plucked me from Scouvrel, throwing me on one shoulder and holding a hand out at waist level. Scouvrel leapt gracefully up, his foot stepping on Rocky's palm like a step stool and landing on his shoulder. The brass needle was already striking the nearest soldier through the neck like the head of an adder lashing out. He plunged it into the next soldier before I could gasp. I missed my bow and arrows.

"My weapons," I gasped.

"So keen to keep your promise, Nightmare?" he asked. "I thought you might delay my murder until I'd at least finished saving your soft skin."

"As opposed to yours which is hard as iron?"

He smiled. "You remember. I'm touched."

I didn't think my eyes could get any wider as Rocky stormed back through the soldiers, his stone feet unrelenting as he charged. Imagine what it would mean to command an army of these golems like soldiers. Imagine how unstoppable they would be.

Nearly as unstoppable as the Knave who had just plucked me from the jaws of torture.

"As formidable as you are, Nightmare," Scouvrel said lightly as he killed another soldier who leapt toward him. "Can I recommend that we wait to retrieve your delightful worldly goods at a later time? I fear that soon they will realize that ranged weapons are the solution to their reach problem and then even Rocky will not be quick enough."

At the back of the crowd, they really did seem to be scrambling for bows and arrows. We were nearly to the edge of the encampment and my heart was in my throat as a knot of men converged, blocking our path.

"And here Rocky might demonstrate the effect of stone on skulls," Scouvrel said as if he were conducting a school lesson. "Rocky?"

"WITH PLEASURE," the golem said. The arm under me moved and then, like the biggest hammer ever made, it came down on the nearest opponent, smashing him in a single strike.

He didn't need to hit again. The soldiers were already retreating, swords and spears held before them like talismans.

"I really would love it if you would reconsider, Rocky," Scouvrel said lightly. "I could increase my offer. I've never before met anyone who so perfectly fit my idea of what makes a proper valet."

"You want Rocky to be your *valet*?" I asked. "You want him to *dress* you?"

"Is that what valets do? I thought they were for general assistance and while I can easily fasten my own buttons," Scouvrel said with a roguish grin, "I find it much harder to crush my enemies' skulls."

"Your buttons are *not* fastened," I commented, pointing at where his shirt hung open all the way to his belt. His wounds had faded to angry red scars twisting through the vines and feathers and though I was trying to hate him with every shred of my being, I couldn't help but melt at the sight of them. He'd borne them for me, after all.

"An oversight," Scouvrel said, looking at me with wide-eyed innocence. "Perhaps as the overseer of order, *you'll* correct my infraction."

"We're leaving my sister behind!" I'd better stick to the matter at hand, or those buttons would drive me to distraction.

"We'll worry about her traitorous skin when we're through this mess, hmm? And when you've seen to my buttons."

I snorted. "How do you plan to get us out of here? These soldiers will be chasing us across the countryside. I've lost my sword – and even if I had it, six months have passed. I don't dare hop between worlds so much if it means losing that much of my time!"

"Only here has so much time passed," Scouvrel said. "It's likely still the Blood Moon in the Faewald."

"How can you know that?" I asked.

He ignored the question.

"Tell me, Nightmare, is there a place nearby with a defensible position and good vantage points?"

"North and to the east," I said begrudgingly. "There's a cave on the top of a mountain trail. Hard to access, known by few, and a good vantage point. You just keep heading uphill until there is no more uphill to go."

"Perfect. Let's go there, Rocky. What do you think?" Scouvrel asked.

"PERFECT."

I sighed. "Why did you let Eckelmeyer see you? You could have fought while being invisible to him."

Scouvrel snickered. "But then he wouldn't have seen the face of the man who will humiliate him slowly until he is nothing but an afterthought."

The soldiers were far in the distance as Rocky strode forward. He was faster than a horse and he could push through the bushes and trees of the forest as easily as walking on a road.

"Why would you bother? What does he matter to you?"

He was silent a long time – so long that I thought he might not answer and then he reached across the top of Rocky's head and grabbed my chin between his thumb and forefinger, looking into my eyes with his huge, feral ones.

"I may never possess you, taunting Nightmare. I may never lay claim to you. But I will tolerate no other man laying claim to you, either."

"Only because you want to kill me yourself," I said dryly. "Don't think I'm fooled any longer by your tempting words. You care no more for me than a hunter cares for a prize buck he's been stalking. He wants the kill for himself – but he won't stay the arrow. I'm a prize to you and nothing more. I'm lucky that we're not near that round door, or you'd have spilled my blood already."

He licked his lips, nervously.

"MOUNTAIN?" Rocky interrupted. I tried to look at where he was pointing, but Scouvrel had my chin held fast.

I slapped his hand away but though he let go of my chin he caught that wrist in a vice-like grip. I felt my lip twist in a slight snarl, but I bit back my annoyance to look where Rocky was pointing.

"Yes, that's the mountain," I said. "The cave is at the top."

I couldn't believe how fast he was. It would take me half the day to walk here from that camp. He was already climbing – straight up, no need for paths or careful trails for Rocky – when Scouvrel pulled me by the wrist until I was so close, I could smell the mint on his breath.

He didn't let me go, just held me there until we reached the entrance of the cave.

"Did you want something?" I asked him as Rocky paused on the edge of the cave.

"OFF," the golem said, leaning forward so that we fell from his shoulders to the rocky ground in a tangled heap.

I bit back a groan. Still, Scouvrel held my wrist, his gaze never leaving mine.

"SLEEP," Rocky said, ambling into the cave. He seemed happy enough.

"If I lift my veil to show you the machinations of my mind, I fear you will tumble with me into the abyss," Scouvrel whispered, his eyes haunted and a little mad.

"If you don't let me in on your plans, Finmark," I whispered, enjoying the way he shuddered when I said his true name, "then I will have no option but to kill *you* before you kill me. Or to run so far and so fast that you'll never see me again."

He swallowed, drawing me close so that we were kneeling together on the cool stone of the mountain, one of my wrists caught in his hand and the tension mounting between us heavy and thick as the rock.

"Bargain with me, Nightmare," he pled, his lips parting as if he were holding his breath.

"Bargain for what? You have nothing I need." That was a lie.

"Bargain with me for your life."

I snorted. "Am I to believe that you will spare my life for the right price?"

His head was already shaking in denial.

"You misunderstand," he said silkily, seductively. "I wish to bargain with you for the taking of your life – for your certain death."

A chill shot through me as his bright, wicked gaze caught mine. It was like he was drinking me in, savoring my terror.

"What makes you think that you have the upper hand here, Finmark?"

The look on his face at the sound of his real name was agony almost mixed with pleasure. I tried not to think about how that made me feel.

"I am the one who has your name." I tugged lightly at his hold on my wrist. "I am the one who has not finalized our marriage. I am the one with the power here."

"I just flew down and saved you from suffering the marring of your pretty face."

"I didn't kill you when I could have," I countered.

"I didn't kill *you* when I could have."

We were both panting now, staring at each other with wide eyes. I leaned forward, hardly knowing why I was letting myself do this. I kissed him, aggressively, possessively, as if I could swallow him whole.

He melted into my kiss, his lips soft, his tongue yielding to me. I gasped and broke away.

That had been a terrible mistake. Who kisses someone who is threatening them?

"What if I asked you to give your life for *me*?" he whispered, his gaze almost timid.

Timidity was not something I expected from him. But I was still reeling from the kiss, my cheeks hot, my pulse thundering in my ears.

"You've been asking for that all along. Correction. You've been demanding it."

He shook his head, his expression torn but he had seized my other wrist when I was distracted and his grip on both was like manacles.

"I want to tell you, Nightmare. I want to tell you everything. It's just ... it's a challenge for me to put myself in a position where I might see all my hopes fail."

"And yet you're asking me to offer my death to you like a grisly sacrifice."

He stood, drawing me up with him, his hands never leaving my wrists. His dark eyes were wide, almost longing.

"I can't see another way. I've looked at it from every angle and I just can't see another way."

"How about trust," I suggested.

"How about you go first?" he said coyly.

I hesitated. I wanted to trust him. But how did you trust a person who said outright that they wanted to kill you? He was a puzzle I longed to solve.

"I stole the book from my sister – the one you led me to."

He was nodding, he stepped forward and I stepped back. My heel met the stone rock face behind me.

"It said a lot of things. About my sister. About me."

It must be killing him to listen silently like that. He always had something to say.

"I thought that maybe capturing her would satisfy the requirements – that it would 'win' her."

"And it didn't," he said. He was leaning so close that I was right against the wall, his breath warming my face. There was no escape from him here. And though I didn't think he was going to kill me right here, it still made my pulse race.

"No." I hated that I sounded breathless. I was not his to master or capture. "It should have. She is, after all, 'the beautiful one.' The one of the earth." I quoted the book to him. "*One born on a single day in two halves. One half for the land. One for the air. One for the rending. One for repair."*

He barked a laugh. "You're misremembering, Allie. Listen carefully to the part you've forgotten:

"For the Earth to rid itself of the air forever, it must only win the half of the Oolag that is of the air – the violent one.

"And for the Sky to take the earth as its vassal, it must only win the half of the Oolag that is of the earth – the beautiful one.

"Your sister is the violent one – the one you must win to ban the Faewald from the Mortal Court forever. You, dearest Nightmare, are the beautiful one – the one that the Faewald wants for the purpose of making the earth its vassal."

"Ridiculous."

"Not at all, Nightmare. It makes perfect sense to me." His voice was burred and thick.

He was so close now that I thought he might kiss me. I swallowed.

"Why do you call me Nightmare?"

"Because you haunt my dreams and make it impossible to sleep. Because you've ruined my happiness and made my life a torturous hell."

"How endearing."

"How inspiring," he breathed. There was only a whisper of air between our lips. He closed the gap, his lips so soft, so respectful – almost worshipful – as he kissed me. "I would not ask for freedom from your torture. I've come to embrace the delicious agony of you. I seek it out, like plunging a knife into my own heart."

This time, when he kissed me, he held my wrists against the rock wall. It was madness to kiss him back. Madness to let him

kiss me when I knew he was nothing but evil. I'd thought I was
immune to the Fae. I had been lying to myself.

"Your stalwart faithfulness to your humanity draws me like
a flame. Your dedication to risking yourself for the vulnerable
has left a mark on me," he breathed. "And yet ... and yet I must
still ask you for the unaskable."

"Why?" I asked, my eyes pricking with tears. Because I
liked him, too. Because he'd saved me again and again even
though he kept pretending he didn't care. Because he'd helped
me save the children even if he acted as if he wasn't helping. I
just couldn't see how that fit with him wanting me dead.

His eyes shuttered closed and his jaw tensed before he finally spoke – as if he was forcing himself to speak, "There was
more to that prophecy, Nightmare. Do you remember it? *'But
if some strange and daring soul desires to bring them both again
as one, to straighten what is tangled and make crooked paths
straight – then only blood will suffice. The blood of both given
willingly to wash us all.'"*

I gasped.

"Are you saying ... you're not saying ..."

"I'm saying that I'm a strange and daring soul. That from
the day I first read that book, I knew what I had to do. And
when Cavariel stole your sister from you, I knew that I had to
do everything in my power to steal you before he could take
you, too. To somehow – and still, I know not how – to convince you to bargain with me. To bargain for a life given willingly. For a death embraced. For the end of what I have come
to crave more than my own existence."

My mouth went dry.

He was earnest. He'd been earnest from the first time I met him lurking in the forest. He was earnest when he tricked me into becoming his through marriage. Earnest when he bought me back with an ear. Earnest even now when he was asking me to willingly die.

"And what of my sister?" I asked through numb lips.

"The other half of your strange soul bond?" he asked with a wry smile. "I had hoped that you could help me with that."

"You thought that not only could I be persuaded to give my own life, but that I could also persuade her."

"I have the utmost confidence that you could do anything you put your mind to, Nightmare. If only you determine to do it."

I was already shaking my head. What he was asking for ...

He sounded regretful when he spoke again. "The worst part, Nightmare, is that I know you will relent. You *will* bargain with me. And when I spill your blood on the stones at the Dread Door, I will spill out my heart with it and all my nights will fade to black and my days will draw out in endless despair."

"Then why do it?" I whispered. "Why ask at all?"

He paused. He was standing so close that I could feel his every breath on my skin. It made the flesh on my arms rise up in goosebumps.

"I was once a child stolen from a family who loved me. I cried out every tear I ever possessed when the Faewald stole me away. They drowned me in the blood of innocents and set me loose as an endless monster. It was a crime against love and life. A crime that has been committed again and again. I want those crimes to end forever. Not just for the sake of mortals – for your kind is no more innocent than mine – but for all of us. I want it more than I want to be happy. I want it more than I want you to live. There are some things that must be. Some things that cannot be denied."

He drew away so quickly that I was suddenly cold.

"I don't expect you to forgive me for what I plan to do but I expect that after some thought, you will agree with me."

And then he slipped into the cave and I was alone and cold, wrapping my arms around my trembling body and wondering when my world had turned to blacks and greys.

Chapter Sixteen

I SHOULD HAVE GONE inside to sleep like the other two. There were bound to be soldiers crawling through the woods looking for us. And my head hurt like a toddler was inside hitting my skull with sticks for fun. But I couldn't rest. I couldn't even sit still. I paced back and forth my hands trembling, nervous energy spilling from me like an over-full cup.

I'd been right all along about how killing my sister was the only way to lock the Fae out of the mortal world forever. And I wasn't going to forget that Queen Anabetha was Fae, too. Maybe all those stories of her beauty and perfection should have made that obvious. After all, even queens had to age, right? But I'd thought the stories of her youth and beauty were just exaggerations, like how you didn't want to tell your mother that she was looking long in the tooth, so you kept saying how beautiful and young-looking she was.

This war between humans and Fae had been started by the Fae – thanks to my sister – and fed by Queen Anabetha who was also Fae. Which meant it was their fault. And unless I wanted to see this same thing repeated again and again on more innocent people, then someone had to stop it. I'd already admitted to myself that I couldn't kill my sister. So that option was out.

But Scouvrel's solution wouldn't work either and not just because I didn't want to die. His plan involved killing my sister, too. Agreeing to it would be as bad as killing her myself.

My mind shied away from thinking about what he wanted. Every time it edged close to that thought it made me quiver with nausea. The memory of his soft kisses tangled in my mind with that feeling of visceral illness.

This was what you got for embracing wickedness, for letting it come close. It ate you up. It sank into your skin, until the only thing left was death. And I was not ready for death.

I needed some kind of alternate plan. Think, Allie, think! You always find a way and it isn't always the way people expect.

Nothing was coming to me. It was as if fear had erased my mind.

I was not at peace with the idea of dying. I wouldn't do that willingly.

And I would not kill my sister. I was no murderer. No matter what she'd done to deserve it, or what she still would do.

Which left me what? A temporary solution?

Maybe everything was always a temporary solution – just enough to get through to the next day forever and ever.

But if you could end evil – or end *some* evil – wasn't that your duty? Even at the expense of your own life?

I shook my head. How many other people had been persuaded to die for that reason only to see their death meant nothing? Wouldn't I be just like them – a fool putting her head willingly into a noose when she didn't have to?

I wished I could know what the right answer was. I wished it would just be perfectly clear instead of muddy as a spring stream.

I'd pulled up my blindfold before I'd realized it, looking out over the rolling forests and rocky hills below. The smoke of Skundton rose into the air in slender columns. The Fae must be living in the houses there. More smoke rose to the south of the town where Queen Anabetha's troops were gathering. What would they be thinking now with their queen gone?

Between the two, there was movement in the woods and on roads so new that the splintered saplings and rough roots torn out to make them still looked pale in the sunlight. I studied the landscape, trying to memorize the changes. It didn't even look like my home anymore. Those fresh clearings and new roads completely changed the landscape. Houses were missing that used to be there, and farms, too. Blackened holes remained where they had once been. And there were new buildings, too. Towers. Walls. What had they done to my home?

I took a deep breath and began to sneak down the rocky path.

I needed to get my sister back.

If there were any answers to be had, they could only be found with her – whether she was willing to work with me somehow or not.

She'd had no pity on my father or her husband. How could I possibly sway her? How could I possibly convince her ... of what, Allie? What will you convince her of when you don't know what you want yourself?

I growled in the back of my throat. This was ridiculous. I had always known what I wanted. And if I was being honest with myself, I knew what I wanted now. That it was impossible, only made me want it more. My feet skidded on loose gravel as I lost my concentration and had to focus on my path again.

I couldn't shake the feeling of Scouvrel's hands on my wrists or the way he looked like he might split apart when I said his true name. I couldn't shake the way his eyes had burned when he admitted that what he wanted was an end to the tangled evil of the Faewald.

But could I really believe that it was a sacrifice for him to ask me to die? He was free with pretty words. It was impossible to know if he was lying.

I froze.

Allie, you're an idiot.

I'd been thinking of Scouvrel as human. I'd been treating him like one of us because his lips and eyes and emotions seemed so very mortal.

Again and again, I forgot that he wasn't mortal. He was Fae.

And the Fae couldn't lie.

I scurried through the woods, quiet as a hunter stalking deer, using all my childhood skills to avoid detection, but my mind was vibrating with the realization that he hadn't been lying to me. That all those words he'd said had to be true.

And that meant that he really did care about me – maybe even more than I cared for him. And he really was ripping apart at the thought of asking me to die.

And he'd sought me out and trapped me and bound me to him for that very purpose.

I wanted to be furious at him. And I was. But what I hadn't expected was the deep well of disappointment mixed with triumph.

Triumph that the way my heart tugged at his every move was reciprocated.

Disappointment that it could never come to anything. That it didn't matter. That he still planned to see me dead.

I shivered.

There's always another way. And I would find it. I would track it. I would pin it like I pinned a target with my arrow. I was still the Hunter.

BOOK TWO

In desperate times, she'll rise, she'll rise.
With Blood Moon high, she'll cry, she'll cry,
On mountain high, she'll break the tie,
In valley low, she'll finally die.
Songs of the Faewald

Earlier in the Faewald:

"*YOU NEED TO GO, NOW,*" *Scouvrel hissed, his eyes flaring bright as he looked back over his shoulder.* "*Take this key. It can get you out of here without an exchange.*"

The woman he spoke to was hidden by shadows, her hands trembling as she took the key, a deep hood cloaking her face.

"*And then what?*"

"*Hide it,*" *he whispered.* "*It came from your people. Let it go back to them. Hide it and keep it until you need it again.*"

"*Malentric will be looking for me.*" *Her voice sounded panicked. A lock of auburn hair slipped from her hood.* "*And so will Maverick. They'll never stop hunting me. They want ... they want ...*"

There was a sob and Scouvrel's eyes made another circle as he studied their surroundings.

"*Enough crying. You need to go now.*" *He plucked a hair from his head, wrapped it around the key and shoved it into her hands.* "*Go. Now.*"

"*But why?*" *she gasped.* "*Why are you helping me?*"

"*Perhaps I still have a conscience, weak as it is, worthless as I am.*"

"*I don't think you're worthless,*" *she said between sobs.*

He sighed and shoved her hard and she disappeared between the rocks.

Chapter Seventeen

I SLID THROUGH THE woods with my blindfold half up and half down. It was a lot farther to go by human foot than it was to go on Rocky's shoulders. Worse, the woods were full of not just people, but of Fae.

In the distance, I heard a roar and what sounded like loosed arrows and singing followed by the howl of a wolf. Dread shot down my spine. If I took a wrong turn in the woods, I could wander right into a skirmish – with no real weapons.

I needed to keep my wits about me. I held my breath each time I moved from cover to cover.

As I wended my way through a thick stand of birch trees, I passed a pair of Fae lounging against the trees, drinking wine from cups crafted of birch bark and laughing together.

"On the morrow, we'll march," one of them said as I hid behind a tree, trying to gauge how best to avoid them. "I tire of these parlor games and I'm ready to drink hot blood again."

"If she hadn't killed Irlip and Farzel, I wouldn't follow her," another Fae agreed – an Autumn-colored- female wearing a spider web dress with a plunging neckline to her waist. I would have been shivering in that outfit, but she seemed not to mind. "But I can respect that level of gore."

"At least she's committed to taking the Mortal Court. It's why we came. With the Lady of Cups vanished, someone had to fill that gap." She sighed. "I long for the Faewald, truth be told. As fun as playing with the mortals is, my soul aches for the Blood Moon and the Wild Hunt. We're probably missing a good one this year. The former Balance will want his revenge."

"What was that?"

I heard a stick snapping across the birch stand from where I was hiding. The Fae all turned to look in that direction and I seized my chance, sprinting through the trees and out of their lines of sight.

Whew. That was a close one, Allie.

I should have asked Rocky to help me, but he did attract a lot of attention and I needed to slip in quietly to get that cage and my things back.

I was careful to keep my path far to the east and away from town. I hoped most of the Fae would be closer to the occupied town.

I clenched my jaw and willed myself to walk forward when a clash of steel broke out behind me, punctuated by high Fae laugher and a strangled scream.

I was nearly to the river when I heard voices. I ducked into a cluster of spruce trees, waiting as they marched by.

"Don't eat that now! We're not going to get dinner for hours and you'll wish you saved it."

Human soldiers.

"I don't care what Eckelmeyer says, he can't keep us from eating. We have rights."

They were gone before I had time to worry about being seen, leaving me shaking with tension. If a pair of guards and a group of Fae made me that nervous, how was I going to manage to deal with a whole camp of my enemy?

I swallowed. Maybe this was a bad idea.

The sound of a twig snapping drew me up short and I spun in place, my vision double from seeing the spirit world and mortal world both at once.

There, on the other side of path, fingers to her lips, stood my mother.

I gasped.

At that moment a scream broke out from further up the path. A scream that sounded suspiciously like the voice of the soldier who had been complaining about eating.

"Run little mortal and let us chase! Make it last an hour this time. The last one was too short!"

Fae laughter rolled out over the screams.

"Mother," I whispered.

She shook her head. Her arms were full of my things – the axe handle. The cage. Everything.

I froze, my eyes eating it all up hungrily.

Running feet beat down the path toward us as screams and wicked laughter filled the air.

My mother placed my bow and quiver deliberately against the tree she was half-hiding behind and set down the glowing book with them. She began to slide into the shadow of the tree.

I took the opportunity to duck behind a tree of my own, looking out over the path just in time to see the first soldier thundered past, wailing. He didn't look right or left. I could have stood right beside the path and he'd never see me, he was so occupied. And with good reason. A Fae lady dressed entirely in red ribbons and nothing else paused right in front of me and flung a pair of silver disks the size of coins at the soldier. She sniffed the air like a buck and tilted her head to the side. I held my breath, only releasing it when she shot down the path after him. The disks looked razor-sharp. She might chase him like that for hours before he died the death of a thousand cuts.

I shivered.

When I looked back toward my mother, she was gone, leaving only my bow and arrows and the book beside the tree.

"You forgot something."

I jumped at the whisper in my ear and spun to see Scouvrel's single raised eyebrow. Was he really in love with me? Did I dare to believe that?

"What did I forget?"

"Me."

"I haven't forgotten you," I whispered. "I simply have no need of you."

It was a lie. But fortunately, I was not compelled to speak the truth as he was.

I hopped over the path furtively and snuck to where my mother had left my bow. Where was she? I scanned the woods, heart pounding, but she was already gone, leaving no trace behind her. Where had she learned to disappear like that?

With a stab of fear, I hoped she hadn't used the sword.

"Why would you leave your only allies to go off into the woods on your own?" Scouvrel hissed as I picked up the bow and quiver.

"Did you see where she went?" I whispered. In the distance, I could hear the screams of the other soldier.

"I was tracking you, evil Nightmare. I paid no attention to the goings-on of lesser Fae and mortals. However they wish to entertain themselves is none of my concern."

I snorted. That was truly unhelpful. I gathered the book up, studying it for a moment – hadn't it been bigger? I remembered it being the size of my whole torso and now it was only the size of my palm. I shook my head and jammed it into the waistband of my trousers.

As I slung the quiver over my shoulder, I saw a note tucked in among the arrows. Carefully, watching all around me, I slipped it out.

"Tracking me to kill me?" I asked coyly.

"No."

I looked up and met his grave eyes. I might as well get this over with. I made my voice hard.

"If you're going to kill me, you might as well do it now rather than drawing it out like a game. Go ahead."

His eyes shone brightly. "Are you offering your life to me? With no bargain at all?"

"Only if you take it right now and end my suspense," I said snidely. If he tried, I'd turn this bow on him in a flash.

"I cannot," he whispered, his hand reached for me and stopped inches before it grazed mine. He let it drop.

"I thought that was all you wanted," I said, unrolling the note. Why was I speaking so sharply to him?

Perhaps it was knowing that he was possibly in love with me but he still wanted to hurt me. It stung all the more than if he'd simply chosen one or the other.

"You are one of the Four. We may not kill each other."

"I didn't think you cared about those rules." And even if he did, if his love was worth anything, wouldn't he break them for me?

"When I say 'cannot' do not mistake that for 'may not.' It is not obedience that binds me, but magic."

I looked up at that. "You literally cannot kill me?"

"No."

"Then why bargain for my death?"

He swallowed, watching me, his breath seeming to freeze in his lungs.

Horror washed over me. "You expect me to take my own life for you?"

His lips half-parted, a guilty look flashing over his face.

I gasped. And to think I'd really been considering whether I could match his affections. I'd really been ... no. No. No.

I leaned in close and snarled, ignoring the way his eyes lit with excitement. "You're the absolute worst, Scouvrel. The worst. There is no one worse than you."

He sagged with relief. "You finally understand. I was beginning to worry you had lost all sense."

Chapter Eighteen

"YES," I SAID DRYLY. "That's clearly the worry here – that *I* have lost all sense. Now, watch my back while I read this note from my mother or someone else might kill me before you get me to your precious door and then what will you do?"

He slid his needle from his scabbard and stood on guard before me, for all the world like a devoted husband and not a wild Fae who was even now hoping I'd kill myself for him.

"You're right," he acknowledged. "If any Fae see you in the Mortal Court, they will hunt you relentlessly. There is still time for one of them to steal your role before you can defend yourself."

I shook my head at their insanity and opened the letter. Why had I ever been lured into thinking there was more to him? If anyone should know that the Fae knew nothing but destruction and death, it should be me.

My mother's letter was written hastily on blue-tinged paper. It smelled of spices in a way that made me think of the Travelers.

It read:

"Dearest Daughter,

"First, let me assure you that we took your direction and those you wished to preserve – including H – are hidden as you requested with the allies you provided. I hope that the knowledge of this sets your mind at ease.

"*I fear to speak more clearly in case this letter is intercepted, and yet it is vital that I communicate these things to you.*

"*Second of all, I have come to discover that actions of mine taken a long time ago set something into motion I did not anticipate. Our current predicament is fully the result of those actions and I am bent on righting those wrongs. I would like to stress that this current time is no fault of yours or your sister's, though both of you have been mired in it, to the polishing and purifying of you and the tarnishing and damning of your sister.*

"*Thirdly, I know a possible solution to the dilemma you face, and I must research just a little more to be certain. You can aid me. And in this way, we can work together to find some third way that does not involve me losing both my daughters. Your father, in his mad rantings, has given hints that the Kinslayer has means to this third way.*

"*And it is in this matter that I need your help. We need to find out what your father learned during his imprisonment in the Faewald. The key is the Kinslayer. Find out what you can. If we can restore your father's mind to him, then perhaps we can glean a full answer. This is vital.*

"*I will not stand to see you dead, Allie. Not for anyone's ambitions or hopes. I will die myself before I allow it. Be safe and be clever and most of all, faithful daughter, use that fine mind of yours to help me solve this puzzle.*

"*Your Loving Mother.*"

How did my mother know about the Kinslayer? And what could she have possibly set into motion years ago?

"I think I could like your mother," Scouvrel said, whispering over my shoulder. "She stirs things up much like a Knave, swooping in here and making demands. Then flying away off to some other mischief. Where has she hidden these people that you wished to see protected?"

"I won't be telling you that," I said acidly. "For all I know, you'd want them dead, too."

"You mistake my desire to save the Faewald for antipathy," he said with burning eyes. "I desire no harm to come to innocents. You should know that since I did not prevent you from saving those you could."

"And yet you want me dead," I said dryly.

"Surely it can not be so distressing to you to think of your death. Your life is so short that your death feels but a blink away."

"Yes, let's just increase the death toll because it doesn't matter when mortal life is so fragile." I was searching the ground for any hint of a trail, but there was no shining trail in my spirit vision and no disturbed leaves or muddy tracks in the real world. My mother had simply vanished. How had she done that?

"You can't increase the death toll, Nightmare. It is always one. One death, for each person. It's fair. It's balanced. In your new role, you must see how utterly just it is."

"Has anyone told you that it's rude to read someone else's correspondence?" I was worried about my mother. I hoped she hadn't used the sword. If she was in the Faewald, she'd be terribly vulnerable. And what was she going to do with the cage? Without my spirit vision, she wouldn't even know my sister was inside, never mind Queen Anabetha. She wouldn't know to feed them or give them water and she couldn't release them without me.

"Has anyone told you that it's my *role* to be rude?" Scouvrel said.

"You and your silly 'roles.' I don't feel this tugging you keep talking about, this forcing into a role," I lied.

"Don't you?" he whispered. "Is that not why you meet my threats with affection and my affection with sworn threats? Are you not trying to even things out, Nightmarish Balance?"

"No," I said shortly. "But I'm done talking about this now. I need to find my mother. She has taken all my magical items."

He snickered. "You're going to wander around a forest full of violent Fae warriors and soldiers looking just so you can try to retrieve your things? I would have thought that you'd be more worried about following your mother's advice."

"What advice?"

"To look into the background of the Kinslayer and what your father may have learned from him."

"And how am I going to do that without a way into the Fae-wald?"

His smile turned devious, "Oh, but you do have a way in, Nightmare. You have me and you have Rocky. And if you'll stop running headlong into danger while we're sleeping, we will get you back to the Faewald. I will even escort you personally to the very heart of the Kinslayer's hold."

"In exchange for what?" I asked.

He paused as if considering, but I knew it was only for effect. His eyes were glittering too brightly not to be holding a secret.

"I want you to agree not to revenge your sister when I take her life. After all, someone has to, and you've already admitted that you can't."

"You want me to exchange my sister's life for a way back to the Faewald?" Why did he still horrify me? How was I not immune to it yet?

"No, sweet Nightmare. I am not asking for permission. Her life was forfeit from the moment she stepped into the Faewald. I am only asking you not to avenge her death. It should be a simple thing. You are not vengeful by nature."

"Aren't I?" I narrowed my eyes to threaten him, but he only laughed.

"Think about it, Nightmare, as you take my hand and lead me to the stone circle."

"We have to get Rocky," I objected.

"He has already agreed to meet me there. He is not pleased that your excursion so rudely ended his sleep."

"Why do I have to hold your hand?"

"Because, despite trying very hard, you are still mostly blind, and we will move more quickly if you trust me to guide you."

I hesitated and his eyes lit with delight.

"Your mistrust is as savory as cinnamon and honey."

"I'd be a fool to trust you," I objected.

"Ah, Nightmare, but you'd also be a fool not to."

He seized my hand, drawing me through the forest like a ghoul drifting through the tangles of trees and brush on a moonless night. They seemed to almost bend from his path as if the forest itself was trying to rid itself of him. His hand was warmer than I'd expected, holding mine in a grip that was both firm and gentle and utterly unexpected from the mercurial Fae. I bit my lip as he led me through the forest. Not just because I was worried for my mother and for the future of our world, but also because I was terribly worried about how my troubles seemed to dim at the press of his palm on mine.

Chapter Nineteen

ROCKY MET US AT THE edge of the forest where it bled out into the rocky mountain plains where the stone circle was raised.

"ARMY," he rumbled.

"They're behind us." I was out of breath from the speed of our hike, but I hadn't fallen even once despite how the world rocked and tilted in my bifurcated vision.

We'd narrowly avoided more conflicts than I could count and there was a sense in the air that something big was brewing. Whoever had finally claimed the leadership of the Court of Nightmares was preparing to bring things to a full battle instead of these scraps of conflict around the town. And with those crossbowmen marching up to join Eckelmeyer and his allies, that meant that the humans were preparing, too.

"NEW ARMY," he said again.

I looked around the clearing. Mercifully, there was no one there, army or otherwise.

"Thank you for waiting for us," I said to Rocky.

"LEAD YOU," he said.

"Sure," I agreed as he shuffled onto the plain, but before I could take a step, Scouvrel spun me around to face him, still holding my hand in his.

"Have you thought about the bargain? Will you stay your hand in exchange for a way back into the Faewald?"

"If I go in there without my sword, I can't get out again without you," I said bitterly.

His smile grew. "Yes, Nightmare. You will be bound to me. Or perhaps, I will be bound to you – serving you as guide and aide even as you attempt to smash my dreams like pottery. It will be a kind of honeymoon I suppose, don't you think?"

"This is what you consider a honeymoon?" I asked. "You shock me at how romantic you are, husband."

His smile was so wide now that I blinked. He almost looked innocent like that.

"Truth or lie," he said silkily, "You will enjoy perusing the Faewald with me even as we flee the Wild Hunt and delve into the depths of the Kinslayer's lair. It will be the most romantic adventure of your life."

"I have no idea," I said, honestly.

"It's the truth, Nightmare. I shall give you a honeymoon for the ages, only bind yourself to me with a simple promise."

"And what promise is that?" I asked.

"That I shall have your last kiss. That in the last moment of your life you shall think of me."

I felt a chill. Why did he have to keep reminding me that he planned to kill me?

"I thought you wanted to bargain for a reprieve from my revenge?" I said, delaying.

"I want to bargain for either ... or both." He looked uncertain for the first time since I met him.

"Truth or lie," I asked, taunting him. "You'll give me the tour anyway."

He winked. "And yet I'd rather have your promise."

I hesitated. But, after all, I was married to him and that meant I could marry no other. I had kissed him, and he'd ruined me with that for anyone else. Anyone else I ever kissed would only remind me of his searing, torrid kisses. I may as well give him this one promise. I couldn't be held to it if it became impossible. It would be very easy to think of him if he was taking my life. Though I doubted those would be happy thoughts.

But more than anything, I *wanted* to give this promise.

Because for all his threats and evil, I found myself longing to be with him all the time. If nothing else, he made the intolerable more entertaining. What could it hurt to bind him to me when I needed him so much?

"Bring us into the Faewald, and I'll make your promise," I said boldly.

His breath caught in this throat and the look of anticipation on his face made me think of a cat watching a mouse's hole.

"Come along, Nightmare. Let's enter the Faewald."

He took my hand again and led me behind Rocky and the three of us stepped into the stone circle.

Scouvrel's smile dripped with mischief as he struck a pose and snapped his fingers.

We entered the Faewald with what I could have sworn was a puff of smoke.

Chapter Twenty

WE STEPPED OUT OF THE circle into the searing white daylight of the Faewald. I ripped off my blindfold before the horrors of the Faewald could penetrate. I didn't need that right now.

I was already shaky and exhausted from the past few days. Who knew what it might take to toss me over the edge of sanity?

The smoke waterfall flowed before us, and the heavy pines swayed in a hot breeze. Striated clouds glowed the dull gold of a sun just arriving. In the distance, a drum beat slow and steady and the ground shook with the beat.

Along the path toward us, a dull clattering sound drifted along the breeze.

"And now," Scouvrel said, tugging off his coat and sweeping it like a cape, "I will have your promise."

My smile matched his.

"I promised to give it in the Faewald. I said nothing about when."

His delight faded, turning to a spiteful frown. "You'd torture me for fun, Nightmare?"

"I'm not the one who started this game."

He leaned in close, "Oh, but you'll finish it, Nightmare. I will see you finish it."

"NEW ARMY," Rocky interrupted.

I looked toward him and froze. In the distance, dust curled up from a winding road – a road that glittered like the scales of a snake as row after row of armored Fae marched down it.

"Which way is the Kinslayer's home?" I tugged at Scouvrel's sleeve.

"Hmmm?" He was watching them, his eyes narrowed.

"Which way do we go? We need to hurry!"

His lips moved as if he was counting.

I huffed.

"FOLLOW," Rocky said.

"Scouvrel?" I pulled at him again, but his eyes never left the coming army. With a huff, I tugged him behind me, following Rocky as he plunged between the trees. I didn't care where he was taking me as long as it wasn't toward those gleaming warriors. I'd figure out how to find the Kinslayer later.

Scouvrel followed me, but he kept his eyes on the distant army as I followed Rocky through the massive trees.

"Where are we going, Rocky?" I asked.

"UNDERMOUNTAIN."

Well, that sounded fairly self-explanatory.

He was outpacing us, his stone feet churning up the ground like hoes in a garden. I tried to speed up, dragging Scouvrel after me. There were white statues in the woods and we dodged them as we ran. I tried not to look at their faces. It gave me shivers to see the dread in their eyes – especially now that I knew what they were – Fae who hadn't started running fast enough when the horns blasted and the Wild Hunt began.

Rocky stopped so suddenly that I almost ran into him. His huge stone hands reached down and lifted us onto his shoulders. And still, Scouvrel was looking behind him.

"What are you staring at?" I whispered urgently.

He shook himself. "They march in the day. Why would they do that?"

"Don't you know? You seem to know everything."

He shook his head, focusing on me again. His eyes were deep wells of smoldering fury. "Promise me, Nightmare. Put me out of my misery and promise me."

His fingers dug into my arm.

"I've already said that I'll make you this promise. But not yet."

He grabbed my hand and lifted it. I tried to pull back, terror slicing through me – but I was stunned when he held my knuckles to his lips and kissed them reverently.

"End my misery. Slow my suffering. Make the promise."

My eyes narrowed. "Is *this* the fourth thing?"

He didn't answer, his eyes blazing into mine.

"Truth or lie." I put an edge to my words. "This is the fourth thing that will complete our marriage bond and tie us together forever. And you are trying to *trick* me into doing it right now."

"Truth." The word sounded like a curse.

I snorted. "You could have told me. And you could have asked. Nicely."

"And be denied?" he challenged. His voice rose an octave as if he was truly upset. "What good would that do me?"

Shadows covered me and I looked up in time to see us running right into a cliff face. I started to scream, but we plunged through without slowing at all.

My scream cut off in my throat. My heart stuttered in my chest, erasing all thought of tricks or marriages.

The other side of the cliff face was a wide earthen corridor filled with creeping roots and chittering creatures. It opened up as we walked, wider and wider and wider until we entered a vaulted room that spread out before us, sloping down and away so that I could see almost to the back of the grand hall under the ground. Everything was carved with blocky, elongated faces, their expressions a monotonous series of fright upon fright.

A pale, soft green light filled the room as if it were trickling down from holes in the ground above the mountain.

Row upon row of stone figures stood shoulder to shoulder with barely a breath between them. They filled the room completely, the lines of them running so far that I couldn't even make out the final figures.

"NEW ARMY," Rocky said.

I gasped.

"Are they asleep?" I asked.

The golems did not move. They did not speak. They did not breathe – but golems didn't breathe.

"THEY WAIT."

"And they are willing to fight?" I asked.

"BARGAIN."

"They want a bargain," I said understanding. "They want their freedom?"

Scouvrel made a sound of disgust from beside me. "I thought *I* was the Knave. Freeing these servants will cause chaos beyond what you can imagine. They are not alive. They are merely dust and magic."

I turned to look at him in the pale glow of the Undermountain. "And what are you, Scouvrel? Are you not dust and magic? If I kill you and leave you here, you'll return to the earth. You're formed of dust. You're of the ground and you'll return to the ground. And yet – inside you lives magic. Magic that gives life to your dust and makes you so much more than just the dust from which you're made. Why can't it be the same for him? For *them*?"

"BARGAIN," Rocky insisted.

"What bargain do you want, Rocky?" I asked.

"VOICE."

"You want a voice for all of them?"

"How could he possibly know what they want?" Scouvrel asked silkily. "Forget this place. It's nothing more than a storage facility. I was distracted before, but I am no longer distracted. Fly away with me and I will take you to the home of the Kinslayer just as I promised."

What would it cost me to give them all voices? Last time that I'd made a bargain for a voice, Scouvrel had flown away and when he returned, he'd come with the certainty that he planned to kill me. That had been a steep payment.

"And if I give them voices, will they fight for me? Will they be my army to fight the Fae and free the Court of Mortals?"

"Any Fae could order them to stop and they'd have to stop," Scouvrel said, rolling his eyes. "They can't be an army for you."

"How do you stop them? With magic? Because you can't fly in the Mortal realm. Maybe you also can't command golems inside it."

"You'd have to get them all into the Mortal Court without being stopped. And who will get you through the circle?"

I turned to him with my best innocent look.

"No."

"YES," Rocky said at the same time.

I held my breath.

"WE FIGHT FOR VOICE."

I could already feel the magic building in me, ready to meet their requests ... if. If I said yes. If I could think of some way to balance their request.

How did you balance the gift of voices to thousands of the Fae's servants? Who did it take from? Who needed something in return? I supposed it took something from the Fae. It took the silent acquiescence of their servants. But they'd taken their labor, so that was already unfair. It didn't really hurt anyone to give them the ability to speak. I tried to let the power flow through me and work to grant them voices but though I could feel it building up, weighing down on me and making my head ache, I could not find a way to channel it.

"Though I try with such energy to persuade you from a dangerous path, yet you still baffle me with your determination to stay your course." Scouvrel shook his head. "You will suffer now until you find a way to fulfill your role. I do not envy you the task. But whatever you do, you should do it with haste. Night will come far too soon, and with it, the Wild Hunt."

I slid down from Rocky's shoulder and looked at his stony face. "Will you wait here with them? I have something I need to do and when I come back, I will have some way to give them all their voices."

"HURRY," Rocky said, swatting Scouvrel off his shoulder and taking his place in the nearest line of golems.

It hurt to see him standing there with the rest, as if he were nothing more than a nameless, faceless creature.

"I'll be back soon," I said, "I promise."

Before I was finished speaking, strong hands gripped me by the waist and soared upward over their pale white heads. As we climbed up through the air, they took on the look of a sea of white flowers under a dark sky. I could have sworn that one was looking up at me.

Chapter Twenty-One

"YOU SHOULD ASK BEFORE you just seize me and carry me away," I said.

"I had to fulfill my role, too," Scouvrel muttered. "It's incredibly hard to be the Knave when the Balance is so out of control. Did you know that the last Balance spent most of his time monitoring magic markets and checking taxation rolls?"

"Faeries have taxes? That seems utterly ridiculous."

"It was an initiative of the former Balance."

Was he holding me closer than necessary? I could feel his warmth as we ascended toward a tear in the rock above us.

"I knew he was cruel, but I had no idea it went that far."

"There are many things I could teach you, Nightmare Balance," Scouvrel crooned. "Just give me that promise."

"You should know by now that I walk my own path, Finmark," I said frostily. "I don't appreciate being manipulated or forced."

I was falling so suddenly that I almost screamed.

And then the breath was knocked out of me as I was caught again.

"Will you *fly* your own path, too? Or are you content to rely on me when you need me and force me away when you do not? I do not like being used, you nightmare of a wife. You terrible, teasing, tormenting creature of a wife."

I could have fallen to my death! That could have been it.

My stomach heaved at the thought and it was all I could do not to vomit all over the golems below us.

"You almost killed me," my voice was a squeak.

"But I didn't. You know I can't."

"It's little comfort."

We dashed through the rip in the mountain and up into the bright white sky. Scouvrel shot up like an eagle, twisting as his dark smoke wings flapped hard to gain height. The air here was clear and cold, and I shivered as it bit my skin like sharp razors.

"The Faewald looks brighter," I gasped.

"You bring newness with you, Changer of Tides, Mover of Moons. Nothing is the same as it was before you stepped into this realm."

We were quiet for a long time as he flew over the sleeping daytime Faewald. Nothing but golems seemed to move below and even as we flew along a white-beached seashore, the fish seemed to swim lazily, their fins flashing under the white light.

I was shocked by how many Fae I saw frozen over the landscape.

"Why weren't there statues before?" I asked.

"Statues?" Scouvrel repeated.

"The Fae frozen in place by the Wild Hunt. They weren't there before. Where were they?"

He laughed. "They're what you want to make your army out of. When the Hunt is over, they'll all be golems. They'll spend the rest of their lives serving us. Remember that the next time the horns sound for the Hunt!"

I swallowed and tried to look at the scenery instead. It was less horrifying. How could I possibly stay good in a world of so much evil? How could I do good when I was the Balance? Was there a way? If there was, I was determined to find it. I thought hard about it as we soared over wonder after wonder, hurrying to the home of the Kinslayer.

"When we get there," Scouvrel said eventually, "We will need to wait for him to leave before we can enter. And that means that we will need to sleep in a nook somewhere and then come out during the Hunt to break into the den of the Kinslayer."

"I could use a rest."

I felt him soften at that.

"What?" Any softness from him felt suspicious.

"I only thought you would object more strongly to curling up in my embrace."

I felt my cheeks growing hot. I'd agreed to *sleep*. Not to ... whatever he meant. My mind stuttered over admitting it even to myself.

"What do you expect from me?" I asked eventually. "I'm married to you. I can marry none other now – I'm yours whether I live to old age or die in the process. Any children I bear will be yours. I will live and die as yours even if I escape your clutches. So, what options do I have? I can't avoid the Faewald. I can't avoid you – because you'll hunt me down. My only option now is to embrace this."

"Or redeem it," he whispered. "Save us, Nightmare. Wash us clean and save us."

"I don't have the power to do that."

"Oh, but you do. You do, if you would only use it." He was pleading. It made me swallow nervously.

We soared over a bay of the sea and a mermaid leapt out of it, her skin gleaming in the bright light. She plunged back into the water again and was lost from view. It was all I could do not to gasp. This strange Faewald still took my breath away.

It wanted to take it away forever.

"Where does the Kinslayer live?" I asked.

"In the Bubblewood," Scouvrel said idly. "It's far too pretty a place for such a role. He ought to live in a house made of skulls and decorated with discarded hopes, but I'm afraid he didn't embrace his role to the extent that he might have."

"I think I can do without the skulls," I said dryly.

"Can you, Nightmare? And here I thought you'd appreciate someone who embraced their role fully. After all, you've embraced yours despite objecting to the wings."

"You know that I haven't. I've only done what I had to do."

His tone was sharp despite his gentle hold on me. "Isn't that true for all of us? And yet you judge us with great harshness."

"Listen. I need an army to defeat my sister and save the mortal world. I found an army. Can I help it if it also fulfills my role?"

"See how the sea flashes here, Nightmare? See how the merpeople rise to the surface and sun themselves? They lure the unwary into their depths to join them in their beds. But mortals cannot breathe water and you drown in the depths. And what happens then? Then, they stake you to the seafloor until the fish eat your flesh away. Isn't that pleasant? It's why they gleam so brightly. They shine with the joy of slaying their enemies. And you think you can defeat *that* with a horde of servants."

"I think I don't need to defeat all of the Faewald if I can just lock it out of the mortal world."

"Selfish little thing. Your black heart cares only for yourself. I love it and despise it all at once."

"Selfish? You think I should take my own life to give you what you want and you call *me* selfish?"

He was descending now along the shoreline to a hidden cove surrounded by steep cliffs. The entrance to it from the ocean was barely wide enough for a person to swim through, but the rim of the pool was edged with many white shells. The shells were larger than the cottage I grew up in and much finer.

"Safety lies in silence now, Nightmare," he whispered.

His feet hit the white sand at the same moment that he drew me along behind him through the maze of shells. He was looking for something. His eyes scanned the shells until he found the right one – one with a smear of earth around the opening. He drew me into it after him.

I had expected a tight squeeze – and it was tight, but it opened up into something I didn't expect. A tiny tidepool filled the bottom of the shell and in a curve above it, a wide ledge the size of a bed was filled with a feather mattress, a jumble of white pillows, and soft, downy white blankets.

"Take off your boots, if you please," Scouvrel said with a mischievous grin. "Actually, you should think about stripping down completely and bathing in that tidepool. You're as tangled as the rest of us."

I felt myself blushing.

"And what will you be doing?"

"Exactly the same thing." He was already stripping down, tossing his ripped and dirty coat in a pile by the narrow shell entrance. "I have clothes hidden in a basket beside the bed. We'll dress in clean attire."

My jaw dropped as he threw his boots to add them to the pile.

"Would you feel better about bathing around me if we were properly married?" he asked as my cheeks flared to new heat. "All you have to do is make one final promise, Nightmare." He leaned in close making my heart pound harder. "Finalize your marriage to me, Alastra Livoto Hunter."

He looked hungry.

I swallowed.

"You married me so you could kill me. Much like Sir Eckelmeyer. You didn't marry me for my looks – you've admitted you don't care for them."

He held up a finger, "And I declared in no uncertain terms that beauty has no inherent value. I'm more than pretty enough for the both of us."

His wink did not help.

I rolled my eyes, but I froze when he tore off his white shirt, revealing the angry red scars wrapped around his torso. My heart stuttered. I couldn't look at them without remembering the price he paid for me. My gaze trailed up to his missing ear. Another reason to hesitate before disregarding him.

"You didn't marry me for my magic or prestige – I have neither of those," I said quietly.

"And what a fool I'd be if I'd married you for those reasons."

I soldiered on. "You didn't marry me because our friendship had grown to the point where you couldn't dream of a life without me."

He laid his finger across my lips and leaned in close to whisper. "But now you lie, precious Nightmare, because I have sworn eternal friendship to you and since the time I swore that, I have not stopped thinking that my life will be over the moment yours ends."

I swallowed. He stepped closer until he could whisper right in my ear.

"Please, Nightmare, end my agony and make us married in truth. Give me your vow, your loyalty, your very self as I have given myself, my heart, my future all to you."

I shivered at his words and somehow, he took that as encouragement. He wrapped his hands around my waist.

"I have never given my heart to another, Nightmare. I have never given my infinitely precious soul to anyone else. Even this body I have kept as my own. And now I offer them to you. Will you still reject me? Will you still refuse me?"

I looked around at the beautiful shell he'd taken me to. Romantic. Enticing. Seductive.

And that was what he was doing to me now, wasn't it? Every nerve in my body screamed to touch him. To run my fingers over those scars and whisper sweet words that teased smiles from his lips. My mind was a traitorous thing.

I stepped back from him.

"You just want me to give myself to you in this romantic white shell like a fool girl who can be swept off her feet. It's another trick. You won't trap me, Finmark," I whispered. "I won't be seduced by you."

His frustrated growl was the last thing I heard before he began to untie his breeches and I had to spin around quickly to face the wall. The splash in the pool beyond was much too loud. No one needed to clean themselves that vigorously. It went on for much longer than needed and then with a growl he left the pool, the water pouring off him in trickles as his wet footprints walked away from me and my heart screamed that I should have just given in.

But I was the Hunter. I surrendered to no one.

Chapter Twenty-Two

EVENTUALLY, THE LOUD water noises were replaced by silence. I waited. The silence drifted into the soft sounds of sleepy breathing.

I risked a glance over my shoulder. Scouvrel lay sprawled across the entire shelf-bed, arms and legs splayed out as if he'd claimed the territory for himself and would surrender it to no one.

One tiny corner of the bed was different – a small pile of clothing lay in that corner. Clothing that was clearly meant for me. I felt my cheeks heating. Even when we were fighting, he'd taken a moment to dig those out for me. I should be ashamed of myself.

Or maybe I should be proud that I hadn't let him turn my head with lies. He was trying to use me. He was as tangled and evil and as wrong as this world he was from and it was only when I forgot that that everything became a jumble in my mind.

It didn't help that he looked so innocent as he slept and so utterly at peace. The lines of his face were smoothed out. He had dressed himself in black leather trousers and a white shirt – which he'd failed to button once again. No stockings. No jacket. And that meant I could see all his scars. They gleamed in the light as if they were trying to remind me that they were for me.

I sighed.

I couldn't leave. So, I'd better wash up.

I undressed furtively, keeping an eye on my sleeping husband. He didn't move even a hair. Carefully, I crept to the edge of the water, bringing my bow and arrows with me. I leaned them against the bed along with the book – I needed to read that again – before I sank into the salty pool of water and began to bathe. It cleaned off the mud just fine, but it made my hair crackly and dry, curling and tangling around me like a bird's nest. I didn't bother re-braiding it when I emerged. I simply slipped to the clothing pile and looked to see what there was.

He'd left me with skin-tight trousers made of an actual snake's silver skin. Pulling them on made me feel as sinuous and sleek as a snake. They adjusted to my every movement with ease. Good. I would need them to pursue the Kinslayer.

The shirt was a different matter. It was white. It draped around me like a filmy cloud. I couldn't deny that it looked nice in a Fae sort of way, but how could it possibly be practical with what was to come? Worse, it had small pink pearls sewn into frothy semi-transparent fabric whorls that made it look like apple blossoms had bloomed right out of the cloth. It was the kind of shirt someone beautiful should wear – someone like Hulanna. It was not the kind of shirt for Allie Hunter – Allie with the plain face and tangled red hair. Allie who was too soft in places where she should be lean and hard.

I put it on with a grimace and turned just in time to see one of Scouvrel's eyes slit open. My mouth opened in horrified rage at the same time that his quiet snickers started.

"You're the worst," I whispered. But he slid over to open up a space for me on the bed even though he was still laughing to himself.

"The very worst of all," I muttered as I took my place in the soft bed.

I was almost mollified by the soft comfort of the feather mattress. I sunk into it like I was resting on a cloud of goose down.

"The clothing suits you," Scouvrel whispered. "You're always half flower and half serpent."

"You're half venom and half trickery," I shot back, but there wasn't much bite to my words. I was enjoying the soft mattress too much.

I was asleep before I knew it.

I awoke to soft whispers beside me. Not singing. More like reciting a poem.

"Soft the broken shadows bend,
Soft the dreams come to an end,
All is restful, all is calm,
All is oil, all is balm,
Dark her lashes on her face,
Dark the spill of frothy lace,
All is beauty, all is light,
All is her, all is delight."

I yawned and the recitation cut off abruptly.

"Awake, my Nightmare?"

He was curled around me, I realized, pillowing my head on his shoulder, his other arm tucked around me possessively.

"I think I am still furious with you," I said, trying to remember why that was, exactly, when he felt so good.

"Your ability to hold a grudge is a delightful thing, Nightmare. And here I thought you could only forgive and show deep compassion. If I had known you could hate so thoroughly, I would have fallen utterly in love with you months ago."

"And now that you know?" I asked dryly. "What now?"

"Ability to hear the truth from me?" he teased.

"Five."

He laughed. "I would have said one. You don't believe me even when I confess the entire expanse of my heart to you. Even when I tell you that I am ensorcelled by you, still you do not believe."

"I will believe you when we find what we need from the Kinslayer."

"Will you?" he asked, his eyes hooded, disguising his emotions.

"I'll give you what you want then."

Now his eyes glowed with yearning. It was hard not to want to give him everything when he looked at me like that.

"I'll give you the promise – the rest of my marriage commitment to you – and I will make the other promise that you want, too. I will promise not to seek vengeance on you for my sister, though I will not raise a hand against her and you will not be able to get her out of the cage without my help – which I also won't give."

His sharply inhaled breath surprised me. He went up on one elbow to look at me. The light in the shell was fading, but the whites of his eyes almost glowed in the dusky light on the shell.

"Still, you think that I work against you, Nightmare. Still, you believe that I am your enemy. I may slay you, but even in that, I am your friend, your ally, your husband."

"Truth or lie," I asked dryly. "You have no idea what it means to be any of those things."

"Lie."

I snorted, pulling away from him and rising to recover the book.

I opened it, letting the bright glow flood over me.

"Trust the untrustworthy.
Follow the blind.
Give that most precious.
Be bold and kind."

"I wasn't looking for meaningless inspiration," I muttered, flipping through the book, but no other words showed themselves.

With a shake of my head, I slipped it into my pocket. It was even smaller now – the size of half my palm.

"I wonder why you're shrinking," I muttered as I retrieved my bow and arrows.

"It has no set size. And it seems to have a mind of its own," Scouvrel said. "They call it the Soothscroll. But it is neither a scroll nor the property of the Sooth."

When I turned back to him, he threw a doublet at me. I caught it, examining the peacock blue item. It was brocaded silk sewn with feathers and slashed with emerald satin with puffs at the shoulders and a high collar. I would blend right in if I walked through the Faewald in such a preposterous outfit. I pulled it on hurriedly and then strapped on my quiver, sliding my bow out of it and carefully stringing it.

"Thank you," I said.

I looked up to see his admiring glance as he shrugged on his own doublet. He was hiding a surprising number of daggers in the midnight sleeves.

"And to think, you claim to have no beauty. No one who says that has ever watched you glare at me with murder in your eyes. It really does bring out their color."

"Should I thank you for saying that?"

"You should thank me for being so hateful that your color rises whenever you see me. Some women would pay for such a pretty complexion."

"Others would just stab you and get it over with," I muttered.

He was beside me before I could gasp. "I wish you would, Nightmare."

I rolled my eyes. "Just get those boots you claim to have hidden and let's get ready. It must be nearly dark enough."

"Your wish is my command ... or at least, it is until you return my name." His tone was overly casual. "Chances that you'll give me that, too?"

"One," I said definitively. I would not be relinquishing the one hold I had over him.

"As I thought. Now, glance outside, Nightmare. Has the Blood Moon risen?"

I glanced outside the shell. The edge of the moon was rising over the horizon. When I looked back and nodded, he passed me a pair of knee-high soft boots.

"These have heels," I said accusingly. "They're entirely impractical."

He looked me up and down as I tugged them on. "I'd say they are fulfilling their purpose with perfect practicality."

I shook my head as I laced them up. Likely, he wouldn't know what 'practical' was if it bit him. I tugged my wild hair into a practical braid as my belly rolled and kicked like a fresh-caught fish.

Here we go.

Time to try to sneak into the Kinslayer's lair while he was away.

Chapter Twenty-Three

THE BLOOD MOON WAS rising and now the blood color flooded half of the rising moon. It gave me a little shiver that went right down my spine, washing down the backs of my thighs all the way to my knees.

"Watch carefully, little Nightmare," Scouvrel whispered and his breath brushed my neck, making me shiver all over again.

We peeked out at the pool before us and then suddenly it was bubbling, the bubbles bursting on top of the water and a strange gas rising up from them. The gas morphed and clustered and then it became specters rising up, up, up from the pool and materializing in the air.

Hulking great orcs with lower teeth sticking out of their fat lips swung their axes with zeal. They were followed quickly by Fae with stag antlers and others with the curving tails of cats. They danced and leapt as they escaped the pond and ran, translucent and jittering, out onto the beach and up the cliff walls nearby. A pair of mounted Fae on the backs of fire breathing horses were next and then pangolins and unicorns and something that looked like a salamander as long as the Skundton inn was tall. They bore on their backs all manner of sneering, laughing, jeering fae armed with bows and blades, fell spears and lances.

A pair of foxes – their tails tied together and lit with ghostly magical fire – came next. Their riders held bows with arrows already nocked, the tips lit with ghastly fire that matched the ones on the foxes tails. It couldn't be real fire – the Faewald couldn't bear that, but this blue, flickering fire looked just as deadly. The foxes leapt forward, each in a different direction. The weaker stumbled and fell only to rise again, pulled along by the stronger.

By the time the dogs emerged, howling and baying in excitement, fear had risen up inside me.

"Calm," Scouvrel whispered. "Deep breaths. They will smell your fear. You must control it."

The dogs sniffed the air, baying, and slathering. There were six of them, large as horse-drawn carts – no, larger! Large as houses. They thundered after the hunters, overtaking them, leaping past and baying into the air, excitement and violence crackling between them like harnessed lightning.

And now their master rose from the bubbling water.

I recognized him immediately. His ears bore their dozen ivory rings. His thorny torso was lashed by a leather harness studded with small bones.

His hound reared up, a snarl ripping from his throat and the laughter of the Kinslayer rose up with the dog's snarl so that they seemed to be one single sound, slicing through the night. The scent of stirred up ponds and cold autumn nights surrounded me, making me shiver as the Kinslayer's eyes glittered with excitement and he sniffed the air in anticipation.

I felt Scouvrel's hand tighten on my shoulder.

Calm, Allie, calm. Let your emotions go in the fire. Take big breaths. No fear, no fear, no fear.

I closed my eyes, trying to breathe normally, drifting in my self-induced calm.

My eyes flickered open in time to see the Kinslayer look in our direction with puzzlement etched into his brow. He shook his head and then galloped away toward where his Wild Hunt was already hot on the trail of some poor unfortunate.

"Hurry now," Scouvrel whispered and we were moving before I could think, dancing from white shell to white shell as we tried to stay masked by the shadows.

I skidded to a stop in front of the bubbling pool but Scouvrel grabbed my arm and tugged me in after him.

"I promised you a full tour. No backing out from our honeymoon now, Nightmare."

And then we were plunging beneath the bubbles. Scouvrel held my arm in an iron grip, tugging me ever downward until I thought my lungs would explode.

He turned to me and laughed, poking my cheek with a free finger and my mouth popped open, the air pouring out in bubbles. He laughed again.

"It's not real water. Just breathe, mortal wife of mine."

My lungs burned and I clawed at his grip as he doubled over laughing again. He swore he couldn't kill me himself and now he was doing it! Panic rocketed through me, stealing all logical thought and I fought with all my might as he laughed so hard that he almost lost his grip on me. I sank my nails into his shoulders and tore at his skin as hard as I could, desperate for air, desperate for life.

My lungs were going to burst. My heart was beating so fast that I couldn't think.

It was over.

This was it.

And he was getting his wish, curse him! I was thinking of him with my last thoughts.

I wanted to stab him.

My lungs gave out and I surrendered to death, gasping in a breath of water, waiting for the depths to take me. I closed my eyes.

Nothing happened.

I gasped.

"Truth or lie," Scouvrel could barely speak through his laughter. "You thought you were going to die."

I gave him my most evil look. And he deserved far worse than that. If my bow hadn't been in my other hand, I would have smacked him thoroughly.

"Truth or lie," I shot back. "You just proved why I shouldn't trust you."

"Because I tell you the truth?"

I couldn't stop the tears that welled up in my eyes any more than I could stop the shakes that seized control of my muscles and left me quivering in his grip.

"Because you didn't tell me before it happened!" I raged. "And because you thought it was *funny* when I thought I was dying!"

"It *was* funny," he said smugly, but he quickly turned it to a look of innocence. "How could I have known that you wouldn't believe me? I've told you again and again that I cannot lie."

If looks could kill, he would be dead a thousand times over. I sucked in a breath and dashed my tears violently from my eyes. He would pay for that. He would pay!

"Come now, my Nightmare, let me give you the honeymoon I promised you." He released my arm from his vicelike grip and offered me his elbow for all the world like a Knight instead of the Knave he was.

My chest heaved as I sucked in deep breaths. No. Not good enough. He couldn't play with me like that.

There was a tension building in my chest. A tension that I was beginning to realize was the Balance within me and before I could think, I was acting on that tension.

"Finmark Thorne, kneel before me and beg my forgiveness."

My hand shot up to cover my mouth even as my eyes grew huge. I shouldn't have misused his name. I shouldn't have ...

He fell to his knees, his eyes sparkling with fury even as he spoke sweetly, "Please accept my apology, worthy Balance. For I am bound to give it and to make obeisance to you for all my sins and indignities."

"Apology accepted," I said breathily but I felt cheated. He should have apologized on his own. He should have given me that much at least.

At the same time, my cheeks flared hot. This compulsion to bring balance would be the death of me. I hated it. I didn't want it. But what could I do? I had acted there without intending to act.

"I told you," Scouvrel said through gritted teeth, "that your role would take you over and force you to act in ways you did not want. You did not understand then that we are all bound and determined by the roles thrust on us, but now, sweet Nightmare, you must see I was right all along."

I nodded, but my mind was racing. I had argued that we made our own choices to accept a role or not, that we couldn't be defined by something that someone else put on us. So why was I allowing this? I hadn't allowed the wings. Maybe, I shouldn't be allowing the compulsion either.

"You should have apologized on your own and then I wouldn't have had to force you," I said weakly.

Scouvrel's expression went tight. "I never apologize. Come now, Nightmare, let's forget this current horror and enter the lair of your enemy."

Was that the best he could do? I supposed I would have to live with it for now.

I took his arm, and we looked together at the underwater home stretched out before us. How in the world would I find an answer in all of that?

Chapter Twenty-Four

THE HOME BEFORE US soared into the water above with walls of something white and woven that looked like the claws of a mighty dragon.

"Tusks," Scouvrel said idly. "His outer walls are made of carved tusks – and some femurs. He carves the story of each one he has killed on one of their bones. And those he holds most dear become earrings and little decorations for that harness he wears. Isn't that nice?"

I shivered. "I thought you said he didn't have a house made of bones."

"I said it wasn't made of skulls."

"That's a fine distinction."

"Oh, don't despair Nightmare. He can't kill you. You're one of the *four*, just like me. He can turn you to living stone. He can set his minions on you. But he cannot kill you himself."

"Why not?" I asked. "It seems silly for the Fae to have rules about who can kill who?"

"Why?" He led me closer to the high, soaring door woven of bone. Above the door, a light hung in what I slowly came to realize was a ribcage. "We have rules for marriage, don't we? Which reminds me, you have forced me to be the moral one in that regard, Nightmare. And moral is not a comely look for me."

"How are *you* the moral one?" I rolled my eyes as I asked him, but if I really did finalize our marriage, I'd be rolling my eyes for the rest of my life.

"I confess, not all my thoughts of you have been chaste."

I felt my cheeks burning. "I don't see how that makes *you* the moral one."

The door was ajar just enough to let a large creature out – like one of those horrific hounds. I felt my steps slowing as I neared it.

"Ah, but if you and I were married, I would not have to be chaste with you and then my thoughts could wander as they wished. But you make me guilty by your delays."

"Yes, clearly that's my fault."

"I knew you'd see sense," he said cheerfully. His cheerful grin turned to an enticing pout. "Now, be a good nightmare and marry me properly. Make an honest man of me."

I snorted. "Even magic couldn't do that, Knave."

"Then make a *married* man of me. That's nearly as good. I think you'd enjoy being married to me. If you think life is fun with me as your friend, imagine what it would be like with me as your full and permanent husband."

"I can only imagine."

"Your imagination is far too mortal. Let me show you instead."

Was he smirking at me?

"Enough," I growled. "We have a world-saving task at hand, limited time, and many foes. This is not the time to tease and trap me. It's the time to show me what a great husband you could be by making yourself useful. I don't have any use for pretty words, but I have a lot of use for action."

He winked. "As you say."

But just like that, his expression transformed to one of concentration and he strode through the water and the open gates even faster than I could.

It was hard to trust the magic of this place that made it possible to breathe underwater and possible to walk without the drag you'd expect from water. Perhaps it was only an illusion of water. I pulled my blindfold up, curious.

I immediately wished I hadn't. This was worse than the stream in the Tanglewood. All around me, still and silent, bodies floated, their feet chained to the ground, their eyes wide and empty. They were ghastly white – as if the waves had leeched all color from their hair and skin and clothes, and the edges of them tangled together.

Bile rose in my throat and I gagged.

The figures were so close – Scouvrel, walking through the water, seemed to barely slide between two floating figures, their open mouths knocking against his shoulders.

Something bumped against my arm. I felt like I was choking. Like I was going to die right here with them and be chained to the seafloor. I clawed at my throat, gagging, unable to breathe.

And then a rough hand tore the blindfold from my eyes.

"Ghastly idea, Nightmare. Why would you want to go and look at reality?" His voice was tight and his hand tugged me after him. I surrendered to his leading. I couldn't shake the feeling that every ripple of water I felt was actually the hands and mouths of the dead against me.

By the time we were well within the high gates and beginning to descend down steps to a basin below, I was shivering so hard that I could barely think.

A slap across my face blinded me with pain. I turned to the threat, heart racing, preparing to defend myself.

Scouvrel smirked. "Got your senses back? Wits about you, Nightmare. You can't hunt if you're steeped in fear."

He was right, I looked down at the dark pit we were descending into, down steps of woven bone.

"This is his home? No wonder he's so intent on dragging everyone else to hell."

"Wait for it ..."

We took another step, and everything changed.

"It's magical," I gasped, as we stepped into the illusion of the Kinslayer's home.

A night sky speckled with bright stars hung wide above us, northern lights dancing across it. And before us, lay a sumptuous living space with stuffed chairs and tufted pillows in fabrics I couldn't have named. They were soft and shining, brocaded and fur-like, studded with bright glass beads or carefully embroidered. The floor was picked out in tiles the size of my fingertips into a mosaic that depicted a Fae lord stabbing a dagger into the heel of a Fae lady who in turn had his foot gripped in her teeth. How very Faewald. Around them, eyes large and bright, were Fae creatures in dramatic poses – unicorns, owl griffins, phoenixes, and even a dragon.

"How did you know?" I gasped.

A wide fire basin held not fire, but a thousand will-o-the-wisps buzzing in a tall lantern three times my height and paned with bubbled glass the color of sunsets.

"I've snuck into most residences in the Faewald a time or two."

There were no walls. The tile floor simply fell away into night sky. But there was a wide bed – carefully made and surrounded by filmy black curtains, a bathing area shuttered with painted screens of constellations, a wide desk with its contents arranged in precise lines, a musical instrument of some kind bearing innumerable keys and long brass pipes and whistles, and a cylindrical bookcase as high as the lantern was, but as it turned, I realized that I never saw the same book twice even when I was certain that it must have come around again.

Even my quiet voice felt like a violation here, so I kept it low. "If I was a secret, where would I be hiding?"

"Somewhere obvious," Scouvrel said. "Somewhere no one would think to look."

"Not a floating island with a blanket?" I said snidely, reminding him of where I'd found his secret.

He growled in the back of his throat.

"If only I had my sword, I could slice my way right to it." But I knew that wasn't true. It would only bring me here and then my wits would have to find the answer. "What could my father have seen here? I thought he was a prisoner of my sister the whole time?"

"Perhaps your sister was dallying with the Kinslayer. Some Fae find the neutral players irresistible."

I scoffed. "That sounds like your imagination."

He leaned in close so that I had to look right in his eyes. "Truth or Lie, Nightmare? You find me irresistible."

I cleared my throat. "Now is not the time for games, Knave. Help me look."

His low laughter taunted me as I moved first to the desk. The items on the desk suggested a very orderly mind. The silver inkstand and quill stood in one corner. A timepiece – priceless in my world – stood neatly in the other corner. A tidy stack of books sat next to the ink and quill. Because of that, it was easy to see that the top of the desk had been carved in careful relief. It depicted a scene that made me swallow uncomfortably.

"I always thought this piece odd," Scouvrel said. "While I deeply admire needless decoration, I have no idea how one would write on so inconstant a surface."

"You've seen this before?" I asked.

"Certainly. Even the Kinslayer is wont to throw a party when the mood suits him. And this desk is a prize of his. As far as I know, it's the only depiction of the haunting story of the Substitute."

"That sounds portentous," I said, opening the drawers.

"Mm."

I looked up, startled. Scouvrel was never tongue-tied. The look of guilt on his face worried me.

"I think you'd better tell me the story," I said as I carefully sorted through neatly arranged papers penned with an exquisite hand. They were all poetry on the theme of nature. An ode to ripples on a pond, the song of the frog in the depths of night, a musing on butterfly wings. Odd that someone whose role involved death spent his time filling his desk with poetry. He'd clearly written all of this. There were even little sketches in the margins of butterfly wings, flowers, moonlit clouds, and constellations.

"It's not really a story for mortals," Scouvrel said lightly. "Why don't I investigate the bed. It looks soft."

I jabbed him in the ribs with my elbow. "Tell me the story, Knave."

He gave a single shouldered shrug as I moved to the next drawer – pen nibs and quills, lined up in order of size. The drawer after that was colored inks in alphabetical order. Not a bottle was out of place.

"It's the story of a mortal woman whose child was stolen by the Fae." His voice was oddly hesitant.

"Typical," I said. "Why did you think I'd find that shocking?"

"Mmm."

There was a long pause as I opened another drawer to find a board with butterflies pinned to it, their names carefully written by each body. I was about to shut it when one of them moved. With a gasp, I pulled out the pins and the butterfly flew – jerkily and with poor rhythm, as if it was in great pain. I watched it flutter up to the ceiling of stars until I lost sight of it.

Eyes wide, I turned my gaze back to the board. The other butterflies were still. Carefully, I removed the pins on the second butterfly and it fluttered to life. I scrambled, pulling pins out with urgency as I freed butterfly after butterfly from captivity.

"I wouldn't have done that if I were you, Nightmare," Scouvrel said lightly.

I would have asked him why, but the answer was already obvious. I could feel the magic welling up in me, compelling me to give a gift to the Kinslayer because I'd taken something from him. I was the Balance now. Even this small act of pity indebted me to him.

Bitterness filled my mouth at the thought.

"Finish the story, Knave."

He chuckled darkly. "As you wish. The mortal woman pursued her child to the Faewald, following his captors all the way to the Dread Doors. There, they had the child laid out on the Blood Stone, ready for the Glory."

"I thought you waited and did it in batches like an efficient autumn slaughter." I kept my tone dry. I was checking the chairs now, looking under them and through their cushions, feeling for loose panels or hidden latches. There had to be a hidden thing somewhere. My mother would not have sent me on a wild goose chase.

"This case was different," he said, following me as I examined the tall lantern and then moved on to the tidy bathing area and then on to the bookcase. "The child had been one of two twins."

I looked up at him, shocked. "And why didn't you want to tell me this story?"

He held up his hands. "I know what you're thinking. Twins. Like you and your sister. You think we were looking for the Oolag. But the child's twin was dead. There could be no Oolag."

"And yet you still took the child."

"Those who came *before* me took the child," he corrected. "And they reasoned that with the child's death, they could cause regular portals to be opened to the mortal world – what you call Star circles or Stone circles. They are the weak points that were ringed with fallen stars to pick them out so no one would ever forget they were there."

"The stone circles weren't always there?" I asked, looking up from the case.

I'd been taking books out at random, shaking their pages to see if anything fell out. They were all useless to me. Novels. Poetry. Fiction. Nothing here was a proper book about the real world, they were all for sheer entertainment. I wanted to scream at that. Who had the time to read all of these? And not only were they fiction, their covers were painted with the most fantastical scenes of Fae riding dragons and Fae flying in huge battles with bright shining lights shooting from their hands or flaming swords as big as they were, of Fae kissing half-snake half-Fae creatures, tangled in each other's arms, or fighting battles with monsters that towered over the mountains. Ridiculous.

"No, this story – the story of the Substitute – is how we made them. Before the stone circles, it was only a fluke of magic that opened the portals, a lining up of the planets in just the right time and place. A trick of magic."

"It sounds like you have no idea how it worked," I said, frustrated as I pulled out book after book only to replace them again. Seriously, who would want to read *this* many books about magic and love?

"We'd never admit to such a flaw."

"So, you tried to secure a permanent opening."

"Yes. And the child was meant to be that opening. They planned to give him the Glory and then slaughter him on the Blood Stone."

"Such lovely family histories you tell, husband."

He hissed. "I tell this at your bidding, you Nightmare of a wife."

"Do go on."

I left the bookshelf. There was nothing there. I was circling the room, searching for any clues, anything I'd missed. The musical instrument held nothing. I pressed the sparkling white keys, jumping back at the blaring noises they made.

Had anyone heard us? I froze, but there was no sound of anyone coming.

Perhaps he kept his secrets where he slept. I wandered to the bed and crouched down to peer under it.

"But his mother offered herself as a substitute," Scouvrel said, his voice heavy as he continued with the story. "Her life for his. Her blood in place of his."

"And it worked?" I asked, pulling my head out from the empty space under the bed to look at his face while he answered.

"It seemed to," Scouvrel said. "But with limitations. One for one. We could enter, but only if we found a human to trade places with us – a Substitute yet again."

"And the child?" I asked, thinking of the desk where a weeping mother was depicted pleading for a baby held up over the head of a devil-like Fae with horns and a tail and a wicked grin.

"Was released to the human world."

"But now the Fae have rushed into the human world without any substitutes. How is that even possible?" I asked.

His voice held violence as he answered. "Now, delectable Nightmare, you are asking the right question. How, indeed? Think about it."

I gasped.

"You don't mean ..."

"If you are thinking of the most grisly thing you can imagine, then you are likely correct in your guess." His words were silk even as they pierced my sense of safety.

"If it was an exchange before – one human into the Faewald for one Fae into the human world, then it meant the death of one of them – the human."

"Yes," Scouvrel said. "A figurative death, or a literal death, but yes. Do you know we didn't figure out that was the exchange? We just thought it was one body in, one body out. It took a human to figure out that it was death that opened the portal."

"Hulanna," I breathed.

"Yes. For every Fae in Skundton right now, there is a Fae who was slaughtered in their place – a sacrifice. A substitute."

"So many ..."

"Remember the logbooks in your sister's room?" Scouvrel asked lightly. "Did you read them?"

"Not really," I said, rifling through the pillows and blankets and searching under the mattress. Still nothing.

"There were names in those books and tallies," Scouvrel said, his voice frosty and hard. "Some of those names were once those I might have called friends."

There was a long silence between us where neither of us moved.

"I absolve you," I said quietly. "If you kill my sister. I will not seek revenge."

"Thank you." His words were a whisper. "But now I need more from you than simply that."

Chapter Twenty-Five

"YOU COULDN'T JUST SAY thank you?" I asked.

The sunset light of the will-o-wisps reflected on his soulful look.

"You know what I'm begging you for. Forgiveness. Complete absolution. The one thing I've seen you give – a magic so strong that no Fae possesses it." His eyes shone with desire.

"I told you I won't seek revenge."

"And I told you that I need more than that."

I sighed. "And I keep telling you that I can't give it to you. You mean to kill me."

"In forgiveness, Nightmare, someone always pays."

I could feel my frustration rising. I sucked in a long breath through my nose. "Yes, but you're asking me to pay twice – first to forgive you and then when I literally pay with my life."

He knelt down on the bed and reached across it to take my reluctant hand.

"Is that so much to ask, Nightmare of my nightmares? Queen of forgiveness? Divine absolver?"

I shook my head, letting my chin drop to my chest so that the loose hair around my face covered my vision of him – protected me from the emotional weight he was putting on me.

"I am none of those things, Finmark. This request is just too much to ask."

"Please."

I stole a glance at his stricken face.

"Please," he said. "I beg of thee. I grovel. I plead. Are you not my salvation?"

"I won't have this argument again and again."

"Then don't have it." He tugged my hand suddenly and I lost my balance, falling into his embrace. "Grant your forgiveness and it will be done."

I shoved myself out of his arms.

It felt wrong to be asked. Like a violation. He was a fool to push me on this. I bit my lip until I tasted blood.

And yet.

And yet I wanted to have the power to please him.

This was just like what the prophecies spoke of. I had the power to bless or break him with this simple word. To rend or to repair.

I could forgive. I could choose to bless and repair instead of rending and breaking.

And with those thoughts, the words my father had muttered by the fire in the Chanter's cottage came back to my mind.

One in two, and two to be one. Rip and mend. Tear and treat. Open and close. Sow and reap.

One in two and two to be one.

I'd assumed he was muttering about the Oolag and the things he'd heard my sister talking about. How the two of us as twins formed one Oolag.

But what if I'd been wrong?

I felt my brow wrinkling as I thought it through. What if he'd heard this story about the Substitute?

"Who tried to kill the child in the story – the one on the Blood Stone?" I asked.

"What?"

"Whose great plan was it?"

"The Kinslayer did the deed. But it was the Soothe who foretold it." His expression was cloudy. "Truth or lie, you're trying to distract me."

"Lie. I'm thinking of something. The Kinslayer opened the circles. And my sister was the one trying to open the door for an army."

"Yes."

"I wonder what he thought of that. There's no communication in this room. No letters. No ledgers. Only poetry and fiction."

"Perhaps he spoke in poems," Scouvrel said wryly.

But that wasn't a bad idea, was it?

What if he *did* speak in poems? What if the poem my father was quoting was from him? What if the two as one and one as two was a reference to this Substitute and not to sisters at all?

I pulled away from Scouvrel and hurried back to the desk, opening the drawer of poetry and flipping through it. Scouvrel joined me, leaning against the desk, flipping through a novel he'd snatched off the bookshelf.

"Why did the substitution work?" I asked Scouvrel. "Could anyone have substituted themselves for the child?"

He shrugged but his words had a bite like he was stung by something. "Who would be willing to die for someone else – unless that person loved them very much? And even then – even that would take a curious degree of faith."

Who, indeed? And yet, wasn't that what he wanted from me? He wanted me to die for him and his people. He wanted me to love them enough. To love him enough.

I tried to force that thought away. Who was he to put all that weight on me?

"Truth or lie, Nightmare," he whispered as I worked. "Once and for all, will you tell me? You aren't willing to give me absolution for your impending death."

"Truth."

He made a disgruntled sound in the back of his throat.

I riffled through the pages of odes to sunset and ballads of the Leaf King and then a single, frayed missive fell out.

There it was in flowing black script:

One in two, and two to be one. Rip and mend. Tear and treat. Open and close. Sow and reap.

Open the circle wide and deep, one to die and one to leap.

Offer now the other side, Keep it open deep and wide.

"She would have started sacrificing humans next," I said.

"I'm sure that's true," Scouvrel agreed, sounding distracted. "Have you ever read one of these stories of unbidden love before? This volume intrigues the imagination."

"I have not," I said shortly. "I'm not sure if you've noticed, but I'm fighting to save humanity."

"How noble," he said dismissively. "This one is called, Agony and Austerity and it seems to be the story of a delightful young woman who only lacks a proper taste for bloodshed."

I rolled my eyes.

"She's dressing in something very drab to go to a party, which, listen to this, this is so droll ... the party has *actual music playing and no one dies at all.*"

He looked up at me with amusement as if this book was so ridiculous that no one could take it seriously.

"Your point?"

His eyes got wider. "Do you mean to say that this is *typical* for a mortal party?"

"Shocking as it might be, Scouvrel, we generally don't kill each other at parties."

"Then why does anyone attend?" He sounded horrified. At least the distraction seemed to have convinced him to stop pushing me to forgive him for killing me in advance. The idea!

"For the dancing. Or the food. Or to be seen."

He preened. "That part I would enjoy."

"I'm sure," I said dryly.

But despite his teasing, something had been stirring within me.

"Scouvrel?"

"Hmmm?" He was fully absorbed in the book. On the cover, someone had painted a woman in a frilly dress being swept off her feet by a man whose shirt had not been buttoned. His muscled torso looked very like the one right in front of me.

"Finmark!"

He shut the book with a snap, eyes focusing immediately on me.

"How are you able to open the portals whenever you please without a substitute or some kind of death?"

There was a whooshing sound and a crack like someone had split a tree in two. The Kinslayer stepped into his home, his eyes blazing.

Chapter Twenty-Six

I GASPED.

"What are you doing in my home?" The Kinslayer took a step forward, drawing a wicked, serrated sword from his scabbard with a *shing* of metal on metal. If 'menacing' was a person, it would be the Kinslayer.

"Have you read this?" Scouvrel asked him, flourishing one hand and pointing at the book he was reading. Somehow, he had the book open again and was reading it without looking up.

"None are welcome here!" The Kinslayer moved to a guard stance that made the thorns along his skin seem to ripple in the sunset light.

"In this scene, the hero is writing a letter," Scouvrel said. "About business. Business! And there are females walking in front of him to show off their lovely dresses. *And still no one has died!*"

"For your trespass, Knave and Balance, you must accept my bargain."

"And now a family is trying to trap a man into marrying their daughter and yet no one has tried any of the traditional ways. No brooms have been left out where they must be leapt over. No one has manufactured an elaborate assassination attempt where the only way to escape involves taking someone's hand. No one has done anything to express interest at all. How is he to know that they are trying to trap him?" Finally, he looked up at the Kinslayer. "Where did you find this?"

"My bargain is this. For the price of leaving, you must give me the chase of a lifetime."

"You can't be more creative than that?" Scouvrel raised a single eyebrow.

"Starting now!"

He leapt toward us and before I could gasp, Scouvrel snatched me up under one arm and was in the air or the water, or whatever it was, flapping on his smoke wings like a duck taking off from a lake.

"It's possible that I overplayed that hand," he said a little breathlessly as we tore up through the illusion of the starry sky and into the water above.

Behind us, there was a howl. Followed by another and another. The dogs were being loosed.

"Can you outfly him?" I asked. Tension roared through me. My head was swimming. Had that really happened?

"Perhaps." His tone warned me that he was up to something.

"Depending on what?"

"Were you about to absolve me back there? Would you have done it if we were given just a little more time? I didn't think you were telling me the truth about that."

"Perhaps," I allowed. My thoughts about him were so confused that I couldn't have said from one minute to the next what I wanted to do with him.

He chuckled and plunged up from the water into the air above. I gasped.

"Quiet now, Nightmare. You are too distracting, and I must fly."

A second howl sounded from behind us and then one of the massive hounds of the Wild Hunt leapt from the water, the Kinslayer on his back. His eyes burned as he chased us, howling, into the night. My heart froze as I met his gaze. He was chase personified. His muscles bunched as he plunged forward, one with the dog he rose so that they lunged and leapt together.

The other dogs flooded up from behind him, spreading out like a herding pack, galloping as they raced to flank us on either side. My breath caught in my throat. We were outnumbered again. There was no hope of escape.

Behind the Kinslayer, I heard the baying of the horn. Dark figures began to emerge one on top of the other. The hunt was upon us.

The Kinslayer aimed something at us. A crossbow?

The wind of the dart barely missing me drew a squeak up from my throat.

"I thought he couldn't kill us!"

"I didn't say anything about maiming."

I squirmed, trying to get at my own arrows.

"Do you want me to drop you, Nightmare? Stop squirming!"

He was flying faster now, but he wasn't gaining height.

"Higher," I said. "Faster."

"Not enough magic," he gasped as our feet scraped the top of the cliff and then we tumbled onto the turf. I bounced across the ground, grunting, trying not to cry out. I hurt all over. Every muscle. Every bone.

I nearly hit the feet of a frozen white stone statue, her eyes wide and hands full of ferns. I rolled past her, wrapping my arms around my face until I came to a stop.

I pulled myself to my feet, examining my bow. It was unbroken. I snatched an arrow from my quiver and readied it.

"Put that fool thing away and run!" Scouvrel said. He grabbed my hand, pulling me.

"But I can fight back!"

"If we could fight back, don't you think I would be fighting?" he snarled. "This is the Blood Moon and none of that will work. We must run and he must chase."

"The shell. We can shelter there," I gasped, as I shoved my weapons back into the quiver.

"I fear not. That opportunity has passed."

We tore across the rocky ground, past clumps of grass so tall and thick that their leaves were as wide as I was. Behind us, far too close, the hound bayed again. It was over the edge of the cliff, the bright-eyed Kinslayer on its back, brandishing the crossbow.

"Why didn't he just drag us to the Dread Doors if he wanted to do that?" I asked.

"He can't. He must chase. It's part of his role – just like Balance is yours."

Which reminded me, freeing those butterflies was still weighing on me. It made it harder to run, harder to think.

"The longer that you deny your role, the harder it is to fight it," Scouvrel explained as he tugged me along under a mushroom as large as an oak tree. It stank of fungus.

I had freed the butterflies. I needed something to counter that. Perhaps if I bound myself.

"Scouvrel," I gasped. "I need to tell you this before it's too late."

"Just don't stop running," he said as we left the cover of the mushroom.

There was a slick sound and when I looked over my shoulder, a crossbow bolt had buried into the mushroom's shaft all the way to the fletching. The end of it quivered, menacingly.

My breath caught in my throat, but I kept running, eyes ahead now, my braid whipping back and forth and lashing the back of my neck like a whip.

I was about to tell him that I absolved him. That I would give him forgiveness even as he tried to kill me. But the words stuck in my throat. Instead, I spoke the weaker, easier promise.

"I will think of you when I die. Yours will be the last name on my mind, your kiss the last I taste."

He spun, twisting me with him and leaning me against the nearest mushroom. His eyes were bright and shocked as the scent of wet earth filled my nose. He kissed me so suddenly that he stole my breath, snatching it into his own lungs. He kissed me as if I was water and he was dying of thirst. As if it didn't matter that we were being chased, only that I had made this vow.

I gasped the moment he pulled away. With his kiss, the weight of my debt lifted.

"You wicked, wicked mortal. You horrific Nightmare of a wife. Who would have thought that in putting me out of my misery you would stab me through the heart?"

"What do you mean?" I asked. Was he angry? His growl certainly sounded like he was, and yet he'd been trying to extract that promise from me this whole time. I'd thought he'd be pleased! I would never understand this man!

I heard the quarrel slicing through the air the second before it pierced my shoulder.

Pain, hot and jagged, filled my mind and I slumped forward. I tried to see what was happening but all I saw was a scrap of Scouvrel's worried face.

"Nightmare! Nightmare?"

And then everything went dark.

Chapter Twenty-Seven

I SURFACED TO THE SOUND of Scouvrel's voice.

"'I must confess that despite your many inefficiencies and disgraces, your mortal flesh, your short life span, and horrific relatives, nevertheless, I have come to adore you,' he said."

Scouvrel's tone changed to a high-pitched squeak. "'Then I am certain you can use those same emotions as salve to your wounds when I dismiss you for a fool.'"

Back to his usual sultry tone. "'May I ask why, with such insolence, I am thrown aside.' Hmmm. A likely question. I asked my own wife the very same and yet she will not forgive my violent spirit any more than your beloved can forgive your cold insults. The game of love is one brought by a difficult bargain."

I moaned. Was he really talking to the characters in the book?

"Nightmare!" I felt something soft on my face and then a gust of air and when my eyes fluttered open, I realized he was kissing my face all over.

"Let me breathe," I moaned to his laughter.

"I had to wait until I found earth-marked shelter to regain my magic – and therefore to kiss your wounds away. I feared I was too late. I never tire of the surprise that comes over how much blood a mortal body can retain. It's a marvel."

"You kissed me and got me shot!"

He shrugged. "What did you expect me to do upon the completion of our marriage, you ghastly thing? Was I to ignore it? So, you were impaled by an arrow. I healed you. End of story."

"Where are we?" I asked, realizing that we were sprawled on something's hide in front of a lantern of will-o-wisps.

The hide had a tangle of horns on one end – something not found in the mortal world – and its hide bore wide, jagged stripes. Above us, even the roof seemed striped and oddly curved, like the inside of a rib cage.

I felt my body. I was dry and whole although my fluffy flowered shirt had a hole in the shoulder and dried blood all over that side of it. Scouvrel, likewise, had a smear of blood on his cheek – likely from kissing me better.

"Our honeymoon suite. Have you never slept in the belly of the beast?" Scouvrel asked distractedly. "Listen to this, 'Oh my sweet soldier, would that you would take me as your own, for your eyes ravish me with every glance and the tips of your fingers spark flames within me.' Now, Nightmare, why is your speech not peppered with such endearments? Surely I am lovely enough to inspire it in you."

"Surely," I said drily. I felt lighter. The pressure from freeing the butterflies was gone. "What happened to The Kinslayer?"

"I fear that I was forced to drag him from his beast by the horns, stab the fearsome cur he rode in the throat and then force it to bear us here to this accommodation."

"Truth or lie? You're joking," I said aghast.

"Lie. I speak only the truth." He looked as smug as a cat with a dead rat under its paw.

"Then why didn't you do that before he shot me?"

He shrugged. "It didn't occur to me then."

I was married to the human-ish version of a cat. He killed without thinking. He made his decisions based entirely on his appetites. He preened for attention and was utterly charmed by his own good looks.

The breath *wooshed* out of me at the thought of the rest of my life walking side by side with this madman.

What had I done?

He'd also saved my life – again.

Against impossible odds – again.

And seemed to be entirely untroubled by it.

Again.

I gritted my teeth with frustration, sitting up in a violent flounce.

"You seem flushed, dear Nightmare. Are you too hot?"

"I'm smeared in my own blood."

"Don't worry, it's still in fashion to wear blood, though it's better if it belongs to someone else. For that reason, my own blood-speckled attire is much *more* fashionable, but I won't tell anyone whose blood is on your shirt if you don't." He winked.

Insufferable.

I took a long, deep breath. There was no understanding him. But I'd better try. After all, it was my fault that we were fully married now.

"Scouvrel," I said carefully. "Are you saying that we are safe and no longer being pursued?"

"Mmm." He was back to his book. "This is surprisingly compelling for a book where no one has died. I'm choosing to believe that they are simply saving the gruesome dismember-ings for the feast at the climax of the book. It's bound to come soon. Look! The heroine has dropped a handkerchief for the hero to pick up and *he gives it back to her without asking for a bargain!* This is simply fantastical!"

I reached out for him, my hand skimming across where his ear once was – the ear he'd offered up for me.

"Husband," I said through gritted teeth. "If you would stop reading for a moment."

He growled. "It's getting to the best part. The regiments have arrived in the village."

"Nevertheless."

He looked up suddenly, setting down the book so quickly that I thought he was going to pounce on me. Instead, he winked.

"Trying to get my attention? You need not do that, Nightmare. You have it exclusively now that we are forever one."

I shivered.

"I see your excitement nearly overshadows my own." His half-lidded smile was almost too much for me.

He'd taken that shiver the wrong way.

"We need to get back to the mortal world," I said, trying not to think about the distracting quality his smile had taken on. "I was trying to ask you when the Kinslayer arrived, how is it that you can travel between worlds without killing someone?"

He chuckled. "I have surprises of my own and my own kind of sacrifice."

"Which is?" I raised an eyebrow and he plucked one of his dark hairs, waving it in front of me.

"For every hair I pluck to open that door, I lose a year of my immortal life."

I shivered again. But he must have thousands of years to give – was it really so bad to ask him for just one more?

"I'm going to need one of those years. Now that we know what my father was talking about, we can go and see my mother, retrieve my things, and get my sister back. We have work to do."

He watched me with a look of wry disappointment.

"I thought you were in a hurry to kill the Hunter girls and that it really couldn't wait," I said dryly. "Where does this sudden patience come from?"

"I thought that perhaps you would like a honeymoon," he whispered, leaning in to kiss my neck where it met my shoulder. I gasped. "A real one."

"I –" I was breathless. I didn't know what to say. I hadn't expected to deal with *this* just yet.

"It's customary in the Faewald to spend the first few weeks after a marriage is finalized in blissful lovemaking. Is this not the same for mortals? Perhaps mortal love is not so strong?"

I coughed awkwardly. If he thought he and I were going to... if he thought ... I shivered again.

"We don't have weeks," I said hurriedly. "I need my army of golems to stop this war. I need to gather my things and find a solution to this problem."

"So," he said regretfully, "No honeymoon?"

"Not until this war is over and my Mortal Court is saved," I said firmly. And then I'd deal with the way my heart sped and my breathing hitched when he kissed my neck like that. I'd remember how he really looked when his glamor was down and call to mind all the horrible things he'd done. That was sure to help reign in my suddenly wild imagination.

"Well," he said coyly. "We can't go out until it's day again."

He turned toward me as if he was about to start kissing me again and I sprang to my feet, hurrying across the corduroy floor – this couldn't really be the inside of a creature, could it? I grabbed at a fur wall hanging and a small hole in the skin wall revealed the world beyond. Daylight flooded the room.

Behind me, I heard Scouvrel's low laugh.

"It's day," I said firmly. "Get those wings ready, husband. You're flying me to the Undermountain."

He was already behind me whispering in my ear.

"Quality of my attempted deception?"

"Two," I said repressively. I had no idea what I was going to do with my brand-new husband and his attempted deceptions and traps and the thought of that both thrilled and terrified me.

Chapter Twenty-Eight

FLYING TO THE UNDERMOUNTAIN took hours. Fortunately, Scouvrel had found us something to eat before we left – a handful of berries and nuts that barely took the edge off my hunger but which he proclaimed to be, "Almost satisfying."

It really was a creature that he had hidden me in – a great, dried out corpse of something he had claimed was a dragon. I didn't look closely enough to see if he was telling me the truth. I didn't want to know. Just thinking of sleeping within the rib cage of something else turned my stomach in ways I didn't want to admit.

We had only just left the ribcage when something smacked me from behind. There was a grunt and then a hiss and I spun to see Scouvrel with his foot on the neck of a orc Fae. The Fae's eyes glittered as they met Scouvrel's. He fought against the pressure to his neck, my husband didn't budge. I swallowed, touching the back of my skull lightly. My head was ringing, but there was no blood.

"Someone is anxious to assume the role of Balance," Scouvrel said and it sounded like a threat. "Care to die for your eagerness?"

The orc grunted. The leather clothing he wore was pale and thin. I didn't want to think of what it was made of.

"What shall I do with him, Balance? Shall I gift you his tongue?"

"I think not," I said carefully. What should I do with him? What would my choice obligate me to do? "But you decide, husband."

His eyes glittered and he shoved his foot harder on the orc's neck.

"Bargain with me."

"Yes," the orc whispered.

But I wasn't listening. I could feel the gift settling on me – I had given Scouvrel something. Somehow, the magic of the Balance would ensure that he would give me something in return. But what?

I missed their bargain, my mind was so intent on thinking about what it might mean. Before I could focus on them, Scouvrel had me by the waist and was leaping into the sky.

I was uncomfortably aware of him as he flew. He'd moved me to ride on his back with my arms and legs wrapped around him. Did I really need to hold him, "tight as a vine 'round a branch" like he'd claimed?

And Scouvrel insisted on reading his book in snatches as he flew.

"How can you read and fly at the same time?" I asked him.

"Explain this to me, mortal," he said. "The father of one girl is forcing her into a marriage with a powerful man – and she is not happy. Why wouldn't she be happy? He chose a good match for her. A man with wealth and power. Is that not valuable to mortals?"

"Is he cruel and indifferent to her?" I asked, feeling awkward about how close my lips were to his ear.

"Invariably."

"Then that's why. Who would want to marry someone cruel?"

"Hmmm. Your sister married a cruel fae, Nightmare."

"And look how that ended?"

He was back to reading. "I'm also confused by this other family. One of the daughters has been given as part of bargain to a distant cousin and *she has refused to honor the bargain.*"

"Shocking."

"My thoughts exactly!"

I laughed bitterly. "In my world, Scouvrel, we are not all pawns in a cruel game of manipulation and deception. We generally marry people for sheer love. And we generally refuse to marry them if we don't like their characters."

His silence went on for a long time.

"Is that what you expected out of a marriage?"

"Of course!"

Again, with the silence. I passed the time watching the trees go by beneath us. It was impossible not to see the beauty of the Faewald. Even tangled around violence and horror, it still took my breath away.

"I have decided that you may love me if you wish," Scouvrel said grandly.

I snorted a laugh. "Your permission means the world to me."

"I thought it might." He sounded contented.

"I think someone needs to teach you sarcasm."

"I've already mastered that one."

"Fine, then you have my permission to fall in love with me, too," I said sardonically.

Now, why had I said that? I shouldn't be getting sucked into his games. I definitely shouldn't be suggesting we could have a real marriage. He was Fae and I was mortal. He loved death and games. I loved loyalty and humanity. He was intent on killing me for the greater good. There could be no happy ending for us.

"I do not require permission to accomplish what I have already wrought," Scouvrel said smugly.

"I have no idea what that means."

"It means I already love you. As the book says, 'most ardently.'"

I choked on something in the back of my throat. He was kidding. Right?

"Immovably. Perpetually. Fully."

"Now you're just listing words," I said, but my voice was a little breathless. Men didn't talk like that. They were affectionate, sure, but I'd seen my father blushing when he whispered something to my mother, and I was relatively certain that even that wasn't this bold of a declaration.

"I read them in this book. Do you like them?"

"They're very descriptive," I said coolly. Best not to believe them. After all, he'd just admitted that he was parroting his silly book.

He spun so fast that I almost screamed. I fell from his back, the air swirling around me. I fumbled for my bow and arrows, trying to make sure I hadn't lost them, but my movement was jerked to a halt as I was suddenly in Scouvrel's arms again, staring right into his eyes.

It took long breaths to still my panic. I'd almost plunged to my death. Again.

"Was that revenge because I mocked you?" I was still a little breathless.

"No," he whispered, his eyes shuttering slightly as he seemed to inhale my fear before he whispered in my ear. "But the book says that men who are in love seize their beloved, drawing them into a tight embrace. I thought that perhaps, it might convince you of the fact that I do not lie. And I am not lying now."

"Impossible," I protested.

His lip curled. "Think as poorly as you like of my capabilities, but know this – I am as capable of loving as any other creature. And my heart has fixed itself on you. I wish to bargain for your affections."

"It doesn't work like that," I said. "You can't negotiate for love. It can only be freely given."

He looked angry. "And you are unwilling to give it to me?"

I almost bust into laughter, but the fury in his eyes kept me quiet. Did he really think he could demand that I love him and that would simply work?

"I'm not unwilling, Scouvrel," I said. "I'm unable. Love is like a plant that grows. I can't give a thing I don't have."

"Then grow it! Now."

"It grows when *you* earn it through acts of loyalty and sacrifice."

He scowled out into the distance. "That is not in the book. There is an impassioned kiss in the book. Perhaps ..."

I pressed a finger to his lips, trying to keep my heart from racing too fast at the idea that he might drop me again.

"Not everything is in that book of yours."

"Hmmm." He sounded disbelieving.

"Now, if you can focus, I have an army to raise and a kingdom to save."

His grunt was a mixture of displeasure and agreement. I almost wished I was still on his back listening to his horrified reactions, but instead, he held me to his chest – almost tenderly – and flew with me in silence to the Undermountain where my army awaited.

I was ready for them. I had the perfect plan.

If only I could come up with a plan to manage my new husband, but try as I might, I could not shove him into a convenient mental drawer any more than he seemed to be able to do that with me. I was going to need to sort out how I felt about him and what I could actually give him or the two of us would tear each other apart.

Chapter Twenty-Nine

WE ENTERED THE UNDERMOUNTAIN and dropped, down, down, down into its depths.

My army was there. Bright white, perfectly sculpted silhouettes in the darkness of the earth.

I could already feel my pulse racing at the thought of harnessing their power.

Scouvrel set me down in front of them but before I could address the still beings, he gripped me by the shoulders and peered into my eyes.

"What you are about to do will change things forever. Think carefully. Is it best to embrace your role to such a degree when you've been trying so hard to avoid it?"

"I see no other way," I whispered, laying a hand shyly on his chest. "Bargain with me."

"For what?"

"I need you to carry my armies out of the Faewald."

"I'm unwilling to pay that price," he said lightly. "Or do you wish to watch me slay a thousand fae for you?"

"No."

"Then the magic will not work."

"Just make a door for me like you did with your hair – just a door. I will pay the price."

I didn't know yet how I would do that. But I had to try.

"And what will you bargain for – what will you give me for the opening of a door."

"I'll give you what you want," I said, feeling panic bubbling up at the admission.

"Your love?" he asked coyly.

I couldn't give him that ... could I? My heart tugged painfully at the thought.

"Absolution," I breathed. "I'll give you that."

His breath caught in his throat.

"As you wish." He took a step back, but his burning gaze never left me. He wanted that absolution. He wanted it so badly that I could have asked almost anything in return for that.

I cleared my throat awkwardly and faced the golems.

"You wish to be my army? You wish to have a voice? Then let us make a bargain." I spoke loudly and my voice carried over the long lines of assembled golems. It felt strange to speak to a silent, still crowd. It was like talking to a mountain. "I will give you your voice right now. And in return, you will march to the Mortal Court and you will help me there. You will fight to quell the war there. You will oppose anyone who takes up arms against one another or against you. You will round up every Fae in the Mortal Court and you will bring them back to the Faewald, under the direction of my emissary." I pointed to Rocky. "If it is agreed. Raise your hand. All who do not raise their hands are free to go."

There was a sound like a landslide and throughout the entire cavern, hands were raised.

I swallowed.

Not a single face had an expression. Not a single eye filled with emotion. And yet, I could feel hope in the room like a note echoing long after it was played.

I swallowed down sudden emotion as I reached for my role and I found it. I would give these golems a voice.

Magic, powerful and heavy, crushed down on me so suddenly that I could hardly breathe, hardly blink. I needed Balance! I needed it now.

Scouvrel was saying something, but I didn't hear him as I fought against blinding pain and urgency.

Now! I needed an answer now!

If I gave them voices, what was fair? What could cancel out so great a gift?

I could take something. But what could I take that had enough value to cancel that gift. The pain was crushing me. I couldn't breathe. I couldn't think. My mind was racing, casting about for any answer I could find.

What if I gave all rocks voices from the smallest pebble to the greatest mountain?

And just like that, the pain was gone, and I was left blinking and gasping like a fish thrown on the bank.

"GET OUT OF ME," the mountain said, booming over us like the roar of a thousand voices.

I gasped and Scouvrel shivered beside us, a look of horror on his face.

"ARMY," Rocky said. "MARCH."

It was all we could do to flee before them as they took a step forward. They were steady. They were certain. They were inexorable.

They were far too fast.

I shared a glance with Scouvrel and we began to run, side by side. Was it possible to outrun the steady velocity of stone feet? We were losing ground quickly.

"They're going to crush us," Scouvrel said between clenched teeth. "Let me carry you."

But before I could answer him, I was flying through the air, landing with a breath-knocking thump on Rocky's shoulder. On the other side of his head, I saw Scouvrel slung over his shoulder, hissing in pain that mirrored my own.

This was insane.

"You're incorrigible, Nightmare," Scouvrel gasped. "Do you know what you've done?"

"Given a voice to the voiceless?" I managed between breath-stealing jolts every time Rocky's feet hit the Undermountain floor.

"You've. *Oof*. Destroyed. *Oof*. The Whole. *Oof*. Game."

I wasn't the only one being jostled with every step.

We broke into the sunlight and the golems raced toward the stone circle, like an eagle dropping through the sky toward prey. They were unstoppable. They were innumerable.

I'd never felt so close to hope as I did right now. What could stand against an army like this? We could win! We really could.

We reached the smoke waterfall and the stone circle before I could catch my breath. I was almost glad that Rocky had been carrying me over his shoulder so that I was facing backward when he finally set me down and my eyes swept across the open forest around the circle.

I began to shake. My trembling growing stronger by the moment.

Scouvrel had told me what was happening. So why hadn't I expected this? The world whirled around me and it was all I could do not to pass out.

Heads on sharpened stakes lined a road leading to the stone circle. They were arranged along each side at perfectly spaced intervals and the line went on long into the horizon – farther than my eyes could see. And from the stakes, their bones had been hung like mad windchimes. The *clacking* and rattling I'd heard when we arrived was a hundred times louder now. I stared down a line of windchimes clattering in the wind, still stained brown with the blood of life, still stinking of death.

Their eyes stared at me, glassy and white.

A scream caught in my throat and I bit it back as I turned to the side and threw up my breakfast.

"The price," Scouvrel said lazily. "I did mention it was steep."

I didn't look at him. I didn't want to see his smug expression. This wasn't a price I wanted to pay. It wasn't a price I was willing to pay.

"EVERYTHING HAS A PRICE." I looked toward Rocky, but he pointed to the stone circle and after a moment, I realized it was one of the stones speaking.

"But this isn't the price I'm going to pay," I told the stone, one hand on my hip.

"EVERYTHING HAS A PRICE," it repeated.

"One in for one out," I said coolly. "Let my army in and we'll bring back every Fae who ever left."

"Take the magic from me," Scouvrel said quietly, locking his eyes with mine. Our bargain. He had remembered. I felt my breath catch in my throat.

There was a long pause and then a sound like something creaking and when I looked into the stone circle, I could see the mountain plain of my home territory.

"Hurry," I said, a little breathlessly. All I could do was hope that the bargain I was making was the one I thought I was making. The bone windchimes and their chilling song made me wonder if anything could ever be that simple.

"Find the Fae in the mortal realm. Round them up. Bring them here. Quell any human or Fae who tries to stop you," I ordered my army of stone slaves. "We hunt."

"YES," Rocky said.

"YES," my army echoed as they began to march, one after another, through the stone circle. With every golem that passed, I felt a heavier weight on my shoulders. It was a debt – a debt I'd agreed to. And if I didn't get the Fae back to the Faewald – and quickly – then the debt would weigh on me until it drove me into the ground.

I swallowed and tried not to panic as the weight increased but it was not easy. Every beat of marching stone feet across the earth, every sight between them of the dead hanging in brutal totems around us, every gasp of breath from my lungs as I fought for control, only fed the spiraling fear I felt.

I had my army. Was I ready for what came next?

Chapter Thirty

WE STEPPED THROUGH the portal to a roar. My eyes opened wide and I scrambled to pull up my blindfold halfway. The double-vision only blinded me for a moment.

From Rocky's high shoulders I could see everything. A rush of Fae running toward us – and between us and the wall, a ragged line of fleeing crossbowmen. They'd arrived. And they were being destroyed.

They were going down faster than I could count, stumbling and falling to the patchy mountain plain and not able to stand up again. Behind them, Fae swords flicked through the air with the precision of a barber, slicing heads rather than hair.

Laughter filled the air between the screams.

My heart raced as I tried to keep my thoughts under control – to assess the situation rather than feel compassion and revulsion wash over me.

The group of Fae attacking this band of humans was small – maybe a hundred all told. My golem army was nearly ten times the size.

"Pass the word," I bellowed to them.

Stone heads creaked as they turned to look at me.

"Every golem from here," I punctuated the words with a powerful gesture of my arm splitting the army into one third. "To here." I swept the arm back to show I meant that full third. "Will sweep to the left around the Fae warriors. Drive them back to the portal. Go!" They were moving before I finished speaking. I turned to the other side. "Everyone from here." My arm shot out but the golems on that side were already nodding, already moving to run to the right and flank the army from the other side.

I stole a glance at Scouvrel whose brow was raised. He hadn't thought they were very intelligent, despite being former Fae. He was clearly wrong.

"The rest," I bellowed, "will spread out here with a gap through to the stone circle. Hold this line. Funnel them into the stone circle. Don't break ranks to let anyone through. Your strength lies in your immobility. Use it."

My voice was already tired as the golems shuffled to move into place, shoved and pushed by one another until they formed a line four golems thick, creating a funnel to the stone circle.

My breath caught as I watched the two sides of the pincher maneuver start to wrap around the laughing Fae warriors. In the distance, they looked up from their game, surprised. Hands flew up as they tried to command the golems – but my warriors were inexorable.

"Remarkable," Scouvrel said, his face stunned. "Utterly re-markable."

"You didn't think I could do it," I said tightly.

"I didn't think anyone could – or should. You'll pay a high price for this, you Nightmare of a Balance."

I wasn't thinking of the price. I was waiting in tense worry as the sweeping charge of my golems finished wrapping around the Fae army.

They stopped. They'd encircled them but now they didn't know what to do. I should have given more orders.

I tried to gesture to them.

"Drive forward! Push them to me!"

Nothing.

There were no humans still standing. They'd been slaughtered before we reached them. My stomach twisted as I scanned the ground where they lay in bloody, mangled heaps.

There were only Fae still standing – confused, irritated, but still as they looked at the ring of stone figures.

Their eyes turned to me and then one of them left the rest and trotted to where the golems ringed them, slipping under a stone shoulder and with a peal of laughter and sprinting for the trees.

I cursed under my breath.

"Bring them to me!" I shouted. "Pass the word to herd the Fae warriors forward!"

But I was too late. Like a storm breaking over the peak of a mountain, the Fae scattered, scrambling between the stone figures of my army with peals of laughter.

I cursed again.

"After them!" I yelled.

It was the wrong thing to say.

My golems rushed after the Fae in every direction, scattering like a flock of birds kicked up by a reckless hunter.

Scouvrel laughed from beside me.

"You can just be quiet," I hissed.

I needed a plan to get them back. I needed help.

"Stop!" I called. "Stop!"

All those within earshot stopped abruptly, their stone feet biting into the lichen-encrusted turf.

I swallowed. That was a start.

"Rocky," I said as calmly as possible. "Can you choose ten others from the group that stopped and put them over equal numbers of those who are left?"

I slid off his shoulders as I spoke.

"YES."

"Please do that," I breathed.

This was a disaster. And it was all my fault.

Chapter Thirty-One

SCOUVREL SLIPPED OFF Rocky's back as the huge golem moved to assemble his leaders. I chewed at my lip as I watched him. I'd just lost most of my army. And the battle hadn't even begun. We needed to get them back – and fast!

"You promised to give me what I wanted," Scouvrel said warily.

"What?" I asked distractedly. My eyes kept drifting to the dead people on the plains. Someone should bury them. Probably me. But after we got the army back together.

"The promise. You said you'd absolve me of your death," he reminded me.

"Oh." I met his gaze, watching his hungry eyes. He wanted this so badly that I could feel it.

I'd promised him this in exchange for opening the stone circle. And I owed it to him. Even knowing that, it felt wrong to give him this absolution but I was too tired to fight it right now. I had too many other things to worry about. Besides, it wasn't like he was going to kill me himself.

"Finmark Thorne," I breathed just barely above a whisper. "I absolve you of all guilt for my death. I forgive your treacherous plans to take my life."

I was such a fool to give him that. Such a fool. I shook my head at myself, my eyes still on the dead crossbowmen. They were dead. I would be dead. We would all be dead and all my best plans to stop that only seemed to delay the inevitable.

Strong fingers took my chin and turned my gaze to his. I blinked back tears.

The look on his face almost shattered me. There was hope there. There was faith. And there was gratitude as bright as the dawning sun, as piercing as a sharp knife, as deeply trusting as a child looking to their parent.

I staggered backward a step, but he stepped forward as I did, his fingers still on my chin, as if there was an invisible tie between us that drew him with my every move.

"Alastra Livoto Hunter," he said, and it sounded like a prayer. "The bargain was not fair. I received far more than I gave."

I shrugged. "Well, you gave me your love with nothing in return."

He looked guilty.

I rolled my eyes. "What now?"

"It was a gift, certainly," he said as if trying to hedge.

"But?"

"But it comes with the determination to steal your affections – which makes it a bargain of sorts. I will steal all your loyalties," and now it sounded like a vow. "And I will rob you of your affections and pilfer the stores of patience and yearning in your heart. By the time I am through plundering you, your heart will be so thoroughly mine that you will not know where your love ends and mine begins. So, don't think I merely give to you. It is not in my nature to give freely. I always give with one hand while the other picks your pocket."

I rolled my eyes. "Of course, you do."

But despite my wry smile and shaking head, most of me was secretly pleased. That had to be the truth. And if it was, it meant that he would be around for a long time as he tried to steal my heart away. And I wanted very little more than to spend all my time with this ridiculous arrogant Fae. Well, I wanted to save the world. And to help my parents. And to deal with my sister. And get my straying army back. But beyond those things, I wanted nothing more than his company and his little speech had made me happy beyond reason.

Beside us, Rocky stopped.

"COUGH."

"Have you appointed leaders?" I asked, never looking away from Scouvrel.

"YES."

"Then we must split up and find the other golems. Each leader and group should add any golems he finds to his group. We'll meet up at the mortal town with as many golems as we can find."

From there, we could plan how to drive the Fae from the town and send the mortal armies back down to the plains by the sea. It was simple enough if I just remembered to plan first instead of acting first. Right?

I breathed out a long, steadying breath.

"YES," Rocky said and raised a hand, snapping his rock fingers with the sound of one rock smacking another. Golems started trotting off in every direction.

I breathed a sigh of relief.

Too soon.

Behind me, the stone circle made a sound like tearing cloth.

I spun in time to see the head of a hound and then his body seem to rise up out of the circle. On his back, the Kinslayer rode, a javelin in his hand. His eyes narrowed at the sight of me and his arm drew back.

"Run!" I shouted and my feet were moving before I'd even turned around again.

Chapter Thirty-Two

WE DASHED THROUGH THE forest with the ripping howls of the Wild Hunt close on our heels. My heart felt like it would explode as I ran, stumbling, twisting to one side only to careen to the next. Within moments Rocky's huge hand grabbed me and threw me onto his shoulder – again. I gasped.

Behind us, another howl began, and the horn of the Wild Hunt sounded.

"I told you there would be a price," Scouvrel said calmly from Rocky's other shoulder. He had his book out again, his eyes fixed on the page.

"The Wild Hunt," I gasped. "They broke into the mortal world! How is that even possible!"

"POSSIBLE," Rocky echoed.

"I can see why you don't believe me when I pour out my heart to you," Scouvrel said, immersed in his book as around us stone figures ran between the trees, knocking branches off and crushing saplings with every step of their stone feet. I swayed as I ducked a pine branch. "The girl in this story has decided she is in love. She met a mortal at a dinner and then saw him ride past on a dashing horse while she was walking, and now she can neither eat nor sleep. And while it is far more likely that her sleeplessness and loss of appetite are the results of an enemy slipping poison into her food, she has concluded that this is love. Is that love to you mortals? Sleepless nights? Nothing to eat? I have given you your share of sleeplessness and hunger, Nightmare."

"I think this book is the worst thing to ever happen to you," I said through clenched teeth as I dodged another branch. "Are we still together, Rocky? Have we lost anyone? I can't tell."

"CAN'T TELL."

"I should have tried one of the books with dragons on it," Scouvrel said. Somehow the branches never hit him. He ducked without looking up. "It would have been more straightforward than trying to figure this out. Everyone is shocked. Apparently, this Mister Wingdam has seen too much of the heroine's pale skin and everyone is scandalized. He can barely think, it has enraptured him so."

"Idiot," I muttered.

"Hmmm. I must admit, Nightmare, that I have not spent much time regarding your ankles. Perhaps when next we find ourselves alone, you will consent to let me study them. If they can do half the things to me that are chronicled here, it will make me utterly your plaything."

"Pay attention, plaything. We're being chased by the Kinslayer."

I risked a look behind me. Between the trees, the bluish hounds leapt and surged. They were right behind us. They were going to catch up.

"Can we run any faster?" I asked Rocky.

"NO."

"The heroines also sigh a lot," Scouvrel said. "Could you try sighing?"

"No!"

We thundered through the trees angling toward the west of Skundton. At this rate, we would be almost to the Chanters' house. Golem feet were fast. Wild Hunt feet were faster.

"We're going to have to go back to the Kinslayer's home," Scouvrel said distractedly.

"Did we miss something?" I asked tightly. I could have sworn that was a drop of slather I'd felt hit my neck. It burned where it hit me.

"This book is just one of three!" Scouvrel said, his voice filled with frustration. "How am I supposed to find out what happens in the third book?"

I reached over and grabbed his collar, "We have lost my army. We are being chased by the Wild Hunt. In the day. That means there are no restrictions on them! And besides that, who cares about the third book? You haven't even read the second!"

He held up a second book. This one had a cover painted with a woman in a yellow, ruffled dress, her head thrown back while a shirtless man kissed her neck.

"I stole two," he said with a wink. "I wish I'd realized there was a third."

I shook my head in astonishment. He had to be kidding. We were running for our lives and he was worried about finishing his story?

"It's not nearly as scandalous as I'd like," he said with a pout. "They are married in this one. It's about their daughter. She's fallen in love with a scoundrel."

"That's wishful thinking," I muttered, letting go of his collar. I needed to think. How could we outrun the hunt?

I couldn't see the other golems anymore, though I still heard them crashing in the trees nearby. I was losing my army bit by bit.

"Can we circle around closer to the town?" I asked Rocky with a gasp as he leapt down a small bluff and landed with a *boom*. "Maybe we could pick up more of the other golems."

"YES."

He spun to the left and plunged forward. I heard a snap and risked a glance behind us. One of the hounds had cracked a tree in half and was throwing it up in the air to catch again.

I shivered, facing forward again just in time to be smacked in the face by a birch branch. My cheek stung.

"You wouldn't believe this part." Scouvrel snickered. "This girl is but fifteen and she is being wooed by a man of forty-two. Ridiculous. His mortal life will be over before hers begins."

"You realize I'm seventeen, don't you?" I asked as I looked ahead for any sign of the other golems. "You're probably at least twenty-seven years older than I am."

"Unlikely. I was a mere child when I was stolen to the Fae-wald and hardly a dozen years have passed since then – and a few of those were spent while you and I were torn from each other as I served the Balance."

"You only served the Balance for six months."

"It felt much longer than that."

"There, Rocky!" I said pointing ahead. "I think I see other golems!"

"YES."

"My sister spent ten years in the Faewald before I saw her again," I reminded Scouvrel as my eyes locked onto the stone forms ahead. "That's at least ten years that you've been there. And you were a full-grown man when I met you."

"Nonsense!" He sounded appalled.

"Who was queen when you were mortal?" I pressed.

The golems ahead had formed a ring around something. But what? This wasn't a part of the forest I was familiar with. We'd strayed far to the east and a little south of Skundton. These golems ran fast!

"Queen? Trying to trick me, Nightmare? There are *kings* in the mortal world, and it was King Aleppo who reigned."

I wracked my brain, trying to remember my history lessons as I strained my eyes. They surrounded a cliff face and a tangle of trees. What had caught their attention?

"Aleppo, Aleppo," I muttered. "Wait. I remember." I began counting on my fingers. "King Aleppo the first, King Aleppo the second. King Aleppo the third, Queen Valentina, Queen Charolona, Queen Christanthem, Queen Analetta, Queen Anabetha. That's eight rulers. Assuming, at a minimum that there are twenty years between each generation, that's almost one hundred and sixty years ago."

There was a thump and I looked back to see him hastily slapping a branch away with a look of shock on his face.

"You didn't notice a hundred and sixty years passing?" I pressed.

He coughed. "I've been busy."

"Clearly."

"Mischief doesn't cause itself."

"I didn't say it did."

A familiar smell filled the air. My belly started to rumble, recognizing it even before I did. My mother's famous stew.

I swallowed.

Scouvrel must have begun to read again.

"She has charmed him with her kind heart and care for a hapless friend," Scouvrel said as he read. "How is it charming to keep a fool alive? Isn't the world better if silly girls die off? That would mean only the clever ones would be left to breed. It's almost as if mortals want to die in horrible ways."

Rocky stopped and I took the opportunity to deal with Scouvrel. I grabbed his collar and pulled his head down toward me. His eyes lit with excitement and his lips parted like he was expecting a kiss.

"You were forgiven in advance for arranging and promoting the murder of someone you claim to love – *me*. Think about that. You were forgiven so very much. Don't you think you can find a little compassion in your heart for someone else? Even someone stupid and silly?"

He laughed. "You don't really expect me to change my character, do you?"

I pulled him closer so I could growl into his face. "I may have married a tangled Fae damned to an eternal hell, but if there's a way to make you human, I'm going to find it. Let's start with practicing compassion."

He winked. "Well, as long as I only have to *practice*."

"Maybe the real thing will come, too."

"I don't think you should expect character from me. Expect instead to adore my beauty and find yourself entangled in my many charms."

If he thought he could charm me out of basic human decency, he was wrong about that.

"If you can't find it in your heart to show a little mercy, then that tells me that you don't appreciate the absolution I gave you," I said in a low voice. "And that means your charms, your looks, all of it – is nothing to me but ashes in my mouth.

Either learn compassion or expect a very frosty reception from your wife."

His eyes widened. "Are you bargaining with me?"

"We're in the mortal world right now, husband," I said with my own wicked smile. "Which means we are playing by my rules. No bargains. Just the truth." I turned my attention back to our situation. "And why have we stopped, Rocky?"

"TROUBLE."

Chapter Thirty-Three

THERE WERE THREE GOLEMS surrounding a cave cut into a steep hillside. I had a vague memory of having been here once before a long time ago, but that was overshadowed by my excitement.

My mother was inside the tight ring of them, holding out *my* sword like a talisman.

"Back, you statues!" she yelled at the same moment that Rocky arrived.

"That's my sword," I said, aghast.

"Allie!" she said as I slid from Rocky's shoulders.

Scouvrel leapt down behind me, grabbing my arm. "We don't have time. The hunt rides!"

"Who is that, Allie?" my mother asked carefully. I opened my mouth but before I could answer she leapt forward, under the outstretched arms of the golems and put her blade to Scouvrel's throat. "He's one of them. Don't move too quickly. Bind his hands while I keep the sword on his throat. Iron burns them."

I smacked her hand, sending her sword away from Scouvrel's throat. He raised a hand to the red weal running across it with a sickened gasp.

"Mother!" I scolded, pulling a handkerchief from my pocket and offering it to Scouvrel. He waved it aside.

"I've taken worse wounds for you, you awful Nightmare," he growled, fixing my mother with a glare. "None of you Hunters should ever be armed."

"Who is this?" my mother asked. She looked like she was seeing a ghost. "I swear, I've seen him before."

"How are you seeing him at all?" I asked.

"He's Fae. I know it." Clearly, she wouldn't be giving me any answers.

I sighed.

"This is Scouvrel, Knave of the Faewald," I said, feeling my cheeks go hot as I made introductions. "And this is my mother – obviously."

"Lovely lady," Scouvrel commented breezily. "I do so admire someone who brands their guests before introductions."

"What is he doing here, Allie?" My mother ducked her head toward me as if she could speak privately despite the fact that Scouvrel was smirking just inches from me. "And what are these living statues?"

"I'm glad to see you, Mom," I said, leaning in to hug her.

She hugged me back, but when I pulled away, she still looked angry.

"I'm happy to see you, too, Allie," her voice was tight. "But not in the company of one of them."

She spat.

"I'm pretty sure that you stole two of 'them' from me, mother." I tried to be gentle. "Where are my sister and Queen Anabetha?"

She held her chin up high, her eyes flashing like she hadn't expected this from me. And why would she? I wasn't Hulanna. I'd never been one to push her.

"We'll talk about that."

"And all my things – my axe handle. My key. My sword," I reminded gently.

"We'll *talk*, Allie. But not before *he* leaves." She pointed with her sword.

I sighed.

"He's with me."

Scouvrel chuckled delightedly.

Behind us, the horns sounded again and my blood turned to ice.

"Whatever bargain you've struck with him, there are loopholes," my mother said coolly. "Recite your bargain to me and I will tell you how to send him away."

"I'm not sending him away." I tried to inject authority into my voice, but it had no effect. "And the Wild Hunt is almost here. We need to run!"

My mother's eyes narrowed and a sudden look of recognition flashed across her face. "Scouvrel. The Knave. I remember you."

"How do you *remember* him?" I felt like my breath had been stolen away.

"Genda," Scouvrel acknowledged with a wink. "You're looking ..."

"You can't lie," my mother said wryly.

"Worn," he said undiplomatically. "Care to bargain for a little glamor to fix that?"

"We don't have time for this!" I said.

"THEY COME." Rocky moved and the other golems followed, leaving the cave entrance and moving toward the forest uncertainly.

She scowled, leaning forward. "Leave my daughter alone! I don't want your kind around my family."

"It's a little late for that, fair Genda," Scouvrel said. "It feels like only the other day I saw you dancing around that circle with pink posies in your hair."

His smirk was mocking, and my mother bristled.

"Wait," I said. "You saw her? A long time ago?"

Scouvrel winked at me.

We didn't have time for this. I shook my head.

"We all need to go. Now. Or hide. The Wild Hunt is right behind us."

My mother opened her mouth to speak but I raised a hand.

"Fetch the cage with my sister and then we need to run."

"Allie," my mother said tightly. "I'm sure you're tired. I'm sure you think you're being reasonable, but Fae are tricky. They will trap you. They will trick you. This hunt doesn't even ride in the mortal world. You have no idea what they're capable of tricking you into."

"This one tricked me into marriage. I bet you didn't expect that," I said tightly, but my eyes were on the woods. The loud crashes were getting closer.

She gasped, looking from Scouvrel to me as he deepened his smirk. He was loving this.

"Now, unless you want to keep arguing about the decisions, I've been making for myself since I was forced to abruptly grow up, we should gather what we need and run before the Wild Hunt overtakes us. Can I have my sword?"

My mother handed it over warily.

"I'll get you your things, Allie, but then we will talk about this," she said, shaking her head as she led us toward the crack in the rocks.

"I'll be right back," I told Rocky. He nodded curtly. "I'll just grab what I need and then we'll meet up with the rest. Can you wait for just a minute?"

"WE WAIT."

"You remember my mother?" I whispered to Scouvrel as we followed her back toward the cave.

"Sure. She came to the Faewald for a day. Pretty young thing. A bit like your sister now that I recall. The Kinslayer was fond of her."

"There's no need to talk about that," my mother said sharply, not even looking over her shoulder as she stepped into the mouth of the cave.

Scouvrel turned to look at me over his shoulder. His mouth twisted as if he was about to tell me a secret and then it dropped open and with a guttural roar, he threw me to the side.

I heard the rocky sound of the golems crying out, their stone fists smashing trees and boulders.

The world flashed by. Sky. Trees. Spirit world. Moss.

I hit a tree.

Pain filled me as my head bounced off the trunk.

Chapter Thirty-Four

I FELT DAZED. WHAT was happening?

My mother was screaming.

I couldn't see her from where I lay, barely sensible.

And Scouvrel – Scouvrel was a blur of action. His needle was out and it flashed in the sun as he fought. His beauty – like a raven with his wings iridescent in the sun – was stunning and he moved with an ease and grace that never ceased to amaze me.

But his opponent was no less graceful. The wave of dark hair the Kinslayer wore covered one of his wicked, glinting eyes as he lunged toward my husband.

I gasped, struggling for breath. I couldn't quite catch a full breath. I couldn't quite get enough air to rise.

I fought against the feeling of falling into airlessness.

The needle glinted, scoring a hit and blood poured down the Kinslayer's exposed chest, spattering across the bone of his harness. He roared, lunging at Scouvrel with a many-headed whip. What had happened to his javelin?

A hound howled so close that I flinched, followed by a snapping sound and a crunch.

My heart was in my throat. Come on, Allie. Get to your feet! Come on.

I leaned forward, coughing weakly on all fours.

"Maverick!" my mother shrieked. "Maverick, stop!"

Who was she talking to? I shook my head, trying not to feel so confused. There was something wrong with my head.

A paw slammed down inches from me, and I looked up just in time to see Rocky lunge to my side. I rolled away and by the time I looked back they were locked in battle, the hound snapping and slavering as Rocky fought with stone fists, cuffing the hound in the nose and then striking for its eye.

Bow.

Where was my bow?

I reached for it, but it wasn't in my quiver. I'd lost it somehow. I scrambled through the tumbled rocks, looking for it.

Another set of golem feet pounded past and my breath caught in my throat as I scrambled back up to my feet. The flurry of the battle was too much to keep up with.

Scouvrel landed at my feet with a *thump*, wicked red slashes across his chest. He coughed and I choked back a scream as red blood bubbled from one of the slashes.

"My husband." I tried to keep my tone calm as I rushed to his side, hands hovering over him as I tried to determine how to help.

"My Nightmare," he gasped. He shoved something at me. "Take it."

"Your novel?" I asked, eyebrows raised.

"Please."

I shoved it inside my shirt. I'd deal with the fool thing later.

"I have the sword," I said, but it wasn't in my belt anymore. I scanned the ground around us. First, the bow and now the sword. Where were they? "Somewhere here. We can flee to the spirit world where you will be safe."

"Your mother," he moaned as he rolled over to hands and knees.

I glanced behind my back and saw her standing there, head held high, chin up. She was looking right in the eyes of the Kinslayer as he stood – stunned – staring back.

"Genda. You were here all along." He sounded shocked. "You've withered. And yet, it seems barely a month has passed since your death."

"It's been seventeen years since I fled your realm, Maverick. I will not return to it without good reason."

"And was I not enough reason to return?" His eyes flashed angrily and his hand shook.

I stood up again, swaying. My mother really did know the Kinslayer.

"How old is that child?" the Kinslayer asked, his arm trembling as he pointed at me. "She is yours, is she not?"

"She's not your concern."

"How old?!" he roared, stepping toward her.

Sunlight glinted off something in the grass and I dove for it. The sword! I leapt to my feet, holding it in both hands. If he thought he could hurt my mother, I'd ...

Scouvrel shot past me before I could take a step, his needle flashing in the sunlight, colliding with the Kinslayer in a massive rolling hit. They flew backward, rolling over the forest floor. I couldn't tell who was winning. The needle flew from Scouvrel's hand, embedding in a tree where it *twanged* in the wood.

A loud cracking sound filled the air, followed by a creak and then I was jumping back as a huge tree fell to hit the ground where I'd been standing. I looked over my shoulder to see a golem on the base of the tree, pinned in place by a slathering hound. The hound lifted his golden eyes to me, his muscles bunching and a growl beginning low in his throat.

A second golem dove, hitting the hound solidly in the side and knocking him off his friend. The hound turned his eyes to his attacker and I stumbled back a step, my foot tangling in something.

My bow.

I reached down and snatched it up, shoving the sword back in the scabbard. My heart was in my throat.

There were still arrows in my quiver. I pulled one out and knocked it.

I could barely keep my hands still as I sought my target.

Scouvrel and the Kinslayer rolled and fought with grunts and roars. I could hardly tell where to aim, but it didn't matter where the arrow flew, did it? It could only hit the Kinslayer after all. Or, if it hit Scouvrel, it would not prove fatal. The arrow would only hit an evil heart.

Loose, Allie! Before it is too late!

Scouvrel screamed and I loosed.

Stay on target! Stay on target!

A figure leapt in front of my arrow, a tree branch clutched in her hand.

No!

My mother.

She stumbled and fell to the forest floor like a dropped basket.

"No!" I screamed, dashing toward her.

Ahead of us, Scouvrel roared, but there was pain in his roar. I caught my mother as she fell to the ground, holding her against me.

What could I do? The arrow was in her chest. Not her heart. Not her heart, right?

My hands trembled as I tried to look. I didn't dare pull the arrow from her chest. It would only make this worse. I knew from long experience hunting that it was very near, or in her heart. Every beat of the heart forced blood out of the arrow hole.

"Hold on, Mother," I said, clutching her to me. I grabbed the edge of her thick skirts and tore, balling up the loose fabric and pushing it against the wound, around the arrow.

Her breath rasped out in awkward gasps as I laid her on the forest floor.

The ground shook as three golems thundered by, chasing a pair of hounds. They whined and snapped, their tails between their legs. We weren't winning ... were we?

Beside me, Scouvrel landed for a second time, his body bouncing off the hard ground. His eye was black, his face pale, and red welts and tears ran across his arms and chest. His jacket and shirt had been torn to shreds. His eyes met mine for only an instant before he whispered.

"I'll be back for you, Nightmare."

A whip snapped through the air and caught his heel, and then he was dragged away, sliding over the loose leaves and needles of the forest floor.

Chapter Thirty-Five

"ALLIE," MY MOTHER GASPED. "Allie, listen."

"I'm listening. I'm so sorry. I love you, Mom."

My breath was coming too fast as my gaze went from Scouvrel being dragged across the ground to my mother's bleeding chest wound, to her face as she spoke, then back to Scouvrel again.

"I love you, too, Allie." She coughed. "You're your father's daughter. Hunter's daughter. You have to know that."

"Of course, I know that," I said through tears. I was shaking all over. What did I do? How did I help her? How did I help Scouvrel?

"You need to take care of him now."

"Yes, of course," I agreed. "You need to rest. I'll find help."

I looked up. Where was Rocky? Where were the other golems?

"He's in the cave between the rocks. So is your sister in that cage." She gasped. "There's so much I need to tell you."

"You should save your energy," I said, putting a hand gently to her brow. She was sweating. "Rocky!"

In the distance, I heard Scouvrel scream.

I tried to catch a glimpse of him, but he was out of sight. A swath of broken trees, blood, and drag marks in their wake, was all that remained. I gasped, my hands shaking as I tried to decide what to do.

I felt a pull – a need to follow – but at the same time, I felt anchored here. My mother's eyelids fluttered.

What should I do? What should I do? Where was Rocky?

I swallowed.

"I'm dying, Allie. I have to tell you," my mother gasped. "You can get your father's mind back. There's a spring in the Faewald. The Spring of Tears. I talked to the elders of the Travelers. They have a legend."

"We'll go together," I said, trying to keep my voice from shaking. "Hold on, okay. We'll go together."

If I took her to the Faewald, I could save her life.

Maybe.

If I struck the right deal as the Balance.

But if I left, that meant leaving Scouvrel to whatever the Kinslayer had in store for him. And it meant leaving my army running loose and vulnerable across the mortal world.

But this was my mother.

She'd always been strong and brave.

She'd always been there for me.

Hot tears spilled down my cheeks.

"More than ever," my mother gasped, "We're depending on you. Don't repeat the mistakes of my youth. Don't trust the Fae. They are monsters. All of them. Even that one you married."

She began to cough, and I clutched her hand.

I needed to make a decision. Now. Before she died and it was too late.

Think, Allie, think.

I heard another scream in the distance – one of pure agony – and one I completely recognized. My heart felt like it was tearing in two. Scouvrel needed me.

My mother needed me.

I looked back and forth from the bloody trail to her and back again.

"Your father," she gasped and then her eyes rolled shut.

"Mom," I gasped.

She wasn't dead. She was still breathing. But I needed to act. I needed to act right now.

I choked on a sob.

In the distance, there was a flash of light and Scouvrel's screams stopped.

I stood up, paralyzed by my mother's body at my feet, the flash of light in the distance, and the hole between two rocks only a few dozen feet away.

Which way should I go?

What should I do?

I choked back a wave of panic and tried to think.

I hadn't even consciously made a decision when my feet were already on the path of broken trees, snatching the needle from the tree and following the carnage. Blood was spattered on trees and bushes and smeared across rocks. Trees as fat as my wrist were splintered apart. Wreckage, everywhere.

I stumbled down the path, my tears slowly stopping and my face hardening. I was ready to fight. I was running out of things to lose.

The path ended in a black burn mark and nothing.

No Scouvrel.

No Kinslayer.

Nothing.

I ran a hand through my hair, looking at the blackened circle as my heart plummeted.

What had I done?

I'd lost them both.

I ran back to my mother on the path, shoved Scouvrel's needle into my belt, and drew the magic sword with trembling hands.

I'd never felt so lost in my life.

Read the rest of Allie Hunter's story in Fae Conqueror: Book Five (and the last!) of the Twisted Fae series.

If you enjoyed Fae Pursuit, please consider leaving a review[1].

Reviews help fellow readers know what books to read and they help me know to prioritize my time and energy to that series. Thank you in advance!

---

1. https://www.amazon.com/review/create-review?asin=B07XLPZTFR

Behind the Scenes:

USA TODAY BESTSELLING author, Sarah K. L. Wilson loves spinning a yarn and if it paints a magical new world, twists something old into something reborn, or makes your heart pound with excitement ... all the better! Sarah hails from the rocky Canadian Shield in Northern Ontario – learning patience and tenacity from the long months of icy cold – where she lives with her husband and two small boys. You might find her building fires in her woodstove and wishing she had a dragon handy to light them for her

Sarah would like to thank **Julie Thomas** and **Eugenia Kollia** for their incredible work in beta reading and proofreading this book. Without their big hearts and passion for stories, this book would not be the same.

Sarah has the deepest regard for the talent of her phenomenal artist Luciano Fleitas who created the gorgeous cover art that accompanies this book. Without his work, it would be so much harder to show off this story the way it deserves!

Thanks also to the Noble Order of Female Fantasy Authors who keep me sane – sort of. And for my beloved husband, Cale and sons Neville and Leif who are endlessly patient as I talk to them about bookish passions.

www.sarahklwilson.com[1]

Follow Sarah to keep up with fun updates:

INSTAGRAM[2]

---

1. https://www.sarahklwilson.com/bridge-of-legends

FACEBOOK[3]
AMAZON[4]
NEWSLETTER[5]

2.   https://www.instagram.com/sarahklwilson

3.   http://www.facebook.com/sarahklwilson

4.   https://www.amazon.com/-/e/B0064MSJRE

5.   https://www.subscribepage.com/brandawareness

Lightning Source UK Ltd.
Milton Keynes UK
UKHW022047160223
417160UK00003B/525